Threefold Desire

Jerry Calonge

Table of Contents

ACT I
The Foundation

CHAPTER 1
FIRST CRACKS

The apartment held the sterile emptiness of a life suspended between what was and what might be. John sat motionless at his kitchen table, the spoon balanced precariously against the rim of his cereal bowl, milk growing warm as minutes stretched into an hour. Framed photographs lay face-down on the coffee table—deliberate casualties of a war he'd been fighting with himself for months.

His phone buzzed against the wooden surface. The notification light pulsed blue, demanding attention he couldn't summon. The wall clock's steady tick marked 7:30 AM with mechanical indifference, each second another step toward a day he wasn't sure he wanted to face.

The morning light filtered through venetian blinds, casting prison-bar shadows across the hardwood floor. Dust motes danced in the golden beams, their movement the only sign of life in the frozen tableau. John's coffee had grown cold hours ago, a skin forming across its surface like ice on a forgotten pond. He'd prepared breakfast out of habit—the same routine he'd followed for fifteen years—but his body had rejected the very concept of nourishment.

Outside, the city was coming to life. Car doors slammed in the parking garage below. A neighbor's dog barked with the enthusiasm of a creature unburdened by existential weight. The garbage truck rumbled past, hydraulics hissing as it swallowed another week's worth of discarded lives. Normal sounds. Normal rhythms. The world was spinning forward while John remained anchored to this chair, this moment, this terrible stillness.

The cereal had turned to mush, individual flakes now indistinguishable from the cloudy milk. Cheerios, he realized with bitter irony—the breakfast of champions and broken men alike. The spoon's weight against the bowl's rim created a fulcrum of tension—the slightest vibration would send it clattering to the floor, but even that small violence seemed beyond his capability.

His reflection caught in the black screen of his phone. Hollow eyes stared back, framed by the stubble he hadn't bothered to shave in three days. When had he started looking like his father? The same defeated slope to the shoulders, the same resignation etched in the lines around his mouth. The genetic inheritance of disappointment was passed down like a family heirloom nobody wanted but everyone received.

The notification light continued its insistent pulse. Blue. Always blue. Like the dress Jennifer had worn the night everything changed, like the ocean view outside their hotel window, The memory didn't come back all at once.

It slipped in quietly, like the tide pulling at his feet before he realized how far he had drifted.

The room had been warm, filled with the soft hum of the ocean just beyond the glass. Curtains moved gently in the breeze, brushing against the walls like they were alive, like they were part of something he hadn't fully understood back then.

Jennifer had been lying on the bed, half-covered by white sheets that never seemed to stay in place. Sunlight spilled across her skin, catching in her hair, turning everything softer… simpler.

She wasn't saying anything.

She didn't need to.

When she looked at him, it wasn't rushed. It wasn't distracted. It was the kind of look that made everything else feel unnecessary.

"You're staring again," she had said, her voice low, almost amused.

John remembered smiling… the kind of smile that didn't take effort.

"I'm trying to remember this," he had told her.

She shifted slightly, making space for him without saying it. Like she already knew he would come closer.

"Then come here," she whispered.

And he did, as if instinct had already made the decision for him.

Her hand found his like it belonged there, her fingers resting against his without tension, without doubt. For a moment, nothing else existed—no expectations, no pressure, no future waiting to fall apart.

Just them. Just that moment.

And somehow… he hadn't realized it was already something he would lose.. Most importantly, like the color of her eyes, the way her stare used to make him smile.

He pushed the thought away before it could take root, but the damage was done. Memory had teeth, and once it bit down, it rarely let go. His chest tightened, the familiar ache spreading between his ribs like spilled wine soaking into fabric. Three years. Three years since he'd seen her face, heard her voice, felt the electric current that passed between them whenever their skin touched, but to John, it feels like it was just a week ago, like the poem from Don't Quit Life

The apartment seemed to mock him with its carefully curated emptiness. A monastery for the emotionally unavailable. She used to move through the space like a hurricane, leaving traces of herself in every corner—a lipstick on the bathroom counter, a hair tie around the bedpost, the lingering scent of her perfume in the air long after she'd gone. He finally reached the stage where only the fondest of memories remained.

Now those traces had been scrubbed away, casualties of his methodical attempt to achieve numbness through erasure. But ghosts don't follow the laws of physics. They persist in the spaces between atoms, in the echo of laughter that never quite fades, in the phantom weight of an absent body in a too-large bed.

The phone buzzed again. Different pattern this time—a call, not a text. The screen illuminated, casting blue light across his knuckles where they gripped the table's edge. Unknown number. Probably spam. Probably someone selling extended warranties or vacation packages to places he'd never visit. He let it ring.

Seven rings. Eight. Nine. The sound filled the apartment like a church bell, marking time he couldn't get back. On the tenth ring, silence returned, heavier than before. The caller would leave a voicemail, and he would delete it without listening to it. Another small act of self-erasure in a life increasingly defined by absence.

A siren wailed in the distance, growing louder before Doppler-shifting into nothing—someone else's emergency. Someone else's crisis was racing through the arteries of the city while John sat paralyzed in his kitchen, unable to lift a spoon to his lips. The irony wasn't lost on him a man who made his living solving other people's problems couldn't solve the basic equation of putting one foot in front of the other.

The wall behind him held a calendar he hadn't flipped through in two months. August still smiled down at him with its promise of summer adventures and vacation plans that would never materialize. Beach houses and barbecues and long drives with the windows down. Futures that belonged to other people, people who hadn't made the mistakes he'd made, who hadn't loved the wrong person at the wrong time in the wrong way.

Or maybe the right person. Perhaps that was the cruelest joke of all—finding exactly what you'd been searching for and watching it slip through your fingers like water. Like time. Like the morning light that was already shifting from gold to harsh white as the sun climbed higher in its relentless arc across the sky.

The spoon finally fell, clattering against the bowl with a sound like breaking glass. Milk splashed across the table, forming abstract patterns that meant nothing and everything. John stared at the mess for a long moment, then reached for a paper towel that wasn't there. Of course, it wasn't there. Nothing was where it should be anymore.

His phone buzzed one more time—a text message. The screen showed a preview of the first few words before going dark again, but those words were enough to stop his heart mid-beat. Enough to make him understand that some mornings, no matter how carefully you try to avoid them, they refuse to be ignored.

The bathroom mirror reflected a stranger wearing his face. John gripped the edge of the porcelain sink, studying the lines that had deepened around his eyes, the way his shoulders curved inward as if he were protecting something already lost. He squeezed toothpaste onto his brush with unnecessary force, the mint burning his tongue as he scrubbed away the taste of yesterday's mistakes.

Water swirled down the drain, carrying foam and regret in equal measure. He forced his mouth into a smile—the practiced expression he'd perfected for passengers who trusted him with their lives thirty thousand feet above ground. The smile faltered, reformed, and held for three seconds before collapsing entirely.

Welcome aboard Flight 447 to Chicago, this is your captain speaking. We're expecting smooth skies today...

The words felt like sawdust in his mouth now, even in memory—fifteen years of those announcements, fifteen years of projecting confidence he no longer possessed. The irony wasn't lost on him—a man who commanded aircraft through storms and turbulence, who had never lost a passenger, couldn't navigate the simple act of looking at himself without flinching.

His hands trembled as he reached for his razor. The tremor was barely perceptible, the kind of thing only he would notice, but it sent ice through his veins. Pilots weren't supposed to have unsteady hands. Pilots weren't supposed to lie awake at three in the morning, staring at the ceiling, wondering if they'd lost more than just their nerve.

The hot water ran out before he finished shaving, leaving him to complete the task with lukewarm streams that matched his mood. He dressed methodically—white shirt pressed to perfection, navy tie knotted with military precision, jacket that still fit the same way it had when he'd first earned his captain's stripes. The uniform was armor; he'd realized years ago. It transformed John Morrison, the man who secondguessed every decision, into Captain Morrison, who projected authority he didn't feel.

The drive to the airport passed in a blur of morning traffic and half-heard radio chatter. His mind wandered, as it often did these days, to the incident that had occurred six months ago. Nothing dramatic—no emergency landing, no lives at risk. Just a moment of hesitation during approach, a split second where the runway seemed to shift and blur before his eyes. He'd recovered instantly, landed perfectly, but the doubt had taken root that day and spread through his confidence like cancer.

The airport terminal hummed with its usual orchestrated chaos. John navigated the crowd with the fluid precision of someone who'd walked these corridors for fifteen years, his pilot's cap tucked under his arm like a badge of competence he no longer believed he deserved. Business travelers rushed past, their urgency infectious but meaningless to him now.

He watched them—these people who boarded his flights without a second thought, who closed their eyes during takeoff and trusted him completely. The weight of that trust had once energized him. Now it felt crushing, a responsibility he wasn't sure he could bear.

The coffee shop line moved with sluggish predictability. He checked his watch—a habit born of countless pre-flight routines—and found himself studying the barista instead of the time. Sarah, according to her name tag, though he'd never asked. Their interaction had evolved over months into something resembling a friendship, if such a thing could exist in two-minute increments between a customer and a server.

"Good morning, Captain John!" Her voice carried that particular brand of cheerfulness reserved for regular customers and those who might offer a tip. "Your usual, or are you finally ready to try something new?"

The question hung between them, loaded with implications he wasn't prepared to examine. Change felt dangerous now, uncertainty his enemy. Even something as simple as ordering a different coffee felt like stepping into an abyss.

John managed what he hoped passed for a grin. "My usual, please."

"The good ones never can seem to catch a hint," she muttered, steam hissing from the espresso machine.

"What?"

"Nothing, your cappuccino is coming right up."

He wondered what hint he was missing, what signal he'd failed to decode. The thought bothered him more than it should have. When had he become so disconnected from the world around him? When did simple human interaction become this foreign?

While he waited, John's attention drifted to a woman at a nearby table. She commanded the space around her without effort—early thirties, strikingly beautiful in a way that made him forget to breathe properly. Designer clothes hung on her frame with careless elegance, and when she spoke into her phone, her voice carried the sharp edge of someone accustomed to being obeyed.

"Valouna, please listen… I'm not trying to control your life. I just think you deserve better!"

The name caught his attention. Unusual, memorable. He found himself constructing a story around it—perhaps a sister, maybe a daughter, someone this woman cared about enough to argue with at eight in the morning. The conversation continued, her tone cycling between frustration and genuine concern.

"I know you think I'm being dramatic, but I've been where you are. I've made those mistakes." Her voice dropped, becoming more intimate despite the public setting. "When Dad got sick, I couldn't be there because I was too busy chasing someone who didn't deserve my time. Don't make the same choice I did."

She ended the call with a frustrated sigh, her fingers drumming against the table surface. The gesture was unconscious, rhythmic—a musician's habit, perhaps, or simply the nervous energy of someone who solved problems for a living. When she glanced up and caught him staring, her smile was polite but guarded—the kind of smile women perfected to deflect unwanted attention.

John nodded in acknowledgment and quickly averted his gaze, hoping she hadn't seen the hunger in his eyes, the way her beauty had momentarily transported him to a dangerous place. He felt ashamed of his interest, of the way his mind had immediately begun undressing her, reducing her to an object of desire rather than the complex person she was.

"Earth to John! Excuse me… your cappuccino."

He collected his coffee and claimed a seat with a clear view of her table, watching as she slipped her phone into her purse and took a deliberate breath, composing herself with the skill of someone who'd learned to hide disappointment. Her hands were steady as she reached for her cup—more constant than his, he noted with bitter irony. He looked down at her long, beautiful legs. "I would kiss them all the way to the part where both legs meet."

The words slipped out before he could stop them, a muttered observation meant for no one, crude and inappropriate. The shame hit him immediately, hot and nauseating. What kind of man had he become? When had his thoughts turned so base, so disconnected from decency?

The coffee tasted bitter on his tongue as he sipped, lost in thoughts that spiraled between desire and self-loathing. He was forty-three years old, successful by any external measure, and yet he felt more lost than he had at twenty-three when the world had seemed full of possibility.

"Morning, John. You look like you're deep in thought?"

Captain Adam's voice cut through his reverie like a rescue flare. The older pilot approached with the easy confidence of someone who'd survived three decades of turbulence—both meteorological and personal. His weathered face wore a smile that had defused countless tense moments in the cockpit.

Adam was everything John aspired to be—respected, unflappable, the kind of pilot younger aviators looked up to. He'd flown through three different eras of aviation, from the wild-west days of deregulation through the post-9/11 security crackdowns to the current age of hyper-automation. If anyone could understand what John was going through, it would be Adam.

"Um… oh, Captain Adam. Just in my imagination, a little bit."

They shared a brief laugh,

One day, this woman would be known to him as Samaya, though he had no reason to know her name at this time. She stood and gathered her belongings with graceful efficiency. She moved like someone comfortable in her skin, confident in ways that John envied. Her phone buzzed as she prepared to leave, and he caught a glimpse of her checking the screen, her expression softening into something warmer.

She glanced back at him once, curiosity flickering in her eyes like a match struck in darkness, before disappearing into the crowd. The moment passed so quickly he almost convinced himself he'd imagined it, but the memory lingered—that brief connection between strangers, the possibility of something more.

Captain Tom chose that moment to stride past their table, his uniform crisp and his demeanor insufferably confident. Tom was everything John used to be and everything he feared he'd never be again—cocky without cause, loud without wisdom, the kind of pilot who made flying look easy because he'd never truly grasped how difficult it could be.

"There goes your best friend," Captain Adam remarked, nodding toward Tom's retreating figure.

The words hit John like a physical blow. His hands tightened around his coffee cup until his knuckles whitened. The casual cruelty of the comment, the assumption that John's dislike was merely a personality conflict rather than something deeper and more complicated.

"Please don't do that. You know I can't stand that guy. This is the fourth time I've told you not to crack those types of jokes. The next time you do it… You and I will stop being friends."

The words came out harsher than he'd intended, but he couldn't take them back. Adam's face registered surprise, then concern. They'd known each other for eight years, had flown together dozens of times, and John had never spoken to him with such venom.

"Relax, iron Mike, don't bite my ear off… I'm sorry."

But the damage was done. Tom's presence had summoned ghosts John wasn't ready to face, memories that clawed their way up from the places where he'd buried them.

The coffee shop began to empty as the morning rush drew to a close. John sat alone now, Adam having departed with awkward apologies that did nothing to bridge the gap that had opened between them. The familiar pre-flight routine called to him—weather briefings, aircraft inspections, crew meetings—but he found himself reluctant to move.

Through the window, he watched planes taxi to their gates, saw ground crews scurrying around aircraft like ants around a hill. It had once been beautiful to him, this ballet of organized efficiency. Now it seemed mechanical, cold, a system that chewed up human beings and spat out statistics.

His phone buzzed with a text from his sister, Laura:

Molly has a recital next Thursday at 7.

Please try to make it this time.

The kids really miss you.

The guilt was immediate and familiar. How many events had he missed? How many times had work taken precedence over the people who mattered most? Molly was seven now, old enough to understand that her uncle's job was more important than her piano lessons and soccer games. Even when Molly made him promise to come to her graduation, he flaked out.

He typed back,

I'll be there. Promise.

But even as he sent the message, he wondered if he'd be able to keep it. The schedule was unforgiving, and his seniority only went so far. There would always be someone higher up the food chain who needed him elsewhere, always another flight to cover for a sick colleague.

The terminal had grown quieter; the morning chaos had settled into the steady hum of midday operations. John forced himself to stand, gather his things, and walk toward the crew lounge, where his first officer would be waiting with weather reports and flight plans. The performance would begin again—Captain Morrison taking control, projecting competence, carrying passengers safely to their destinations.

But as he walked, he couldn't shake the image of the woman from the coffee shop, the way she'd looked at him with those curious eyes. For a moment, he'd felt seen, not as a pilot or a captain or a failed ex-husband and uncle, but as a man. The feeling was terrifying and intoxicating in equal measure.

What if? He thought, and immediately pushed the question away. What-ifs were dangerous for pilots, distractions that could turn routine flights into disasters. But the question lingered as he approached the gate, as he began the ritual of pre-flight preparation, and as he smiled at passengers, assuring them of smooth skies ahead.

What if he'd been brave enough to introduce himself? What if she'd smiled back, genuinely this time? What if there were still possibilities in his life beyond the narrow corridor between takeoff and landing?

The answers would have to wait. Flight 447 to Chicago was boarding, and Captain Morrison had work to do. But somewhere beneath the uniform, John Morrison was beginning to wonder if it might be time to learn how to fly again—not just aircraft, but himself.

Three Years Earlier

The apartment had been different then—warmer, filled with the accumulated detritus of a shared life. Photographs smiled from every surface: John and Jennifer on their honeymoon in Santorini, laughing at some forgotten joke; their wedding day, her dress a cascade of white silk against the Chicago skyline; casual snapshots from better times when touching each other had felt natural rather than negotiated. The walls held the scent of Jennifer's perfume mixed with coffee and contentment, though lately the contentment felt forced, manufactured through routine rather than genuine affection.

John sat across from his wife at their dining table, picking at the salmon she'd prepared with her usual precision. Everything Jennifer did carried that quality—deliberate, thoughtful, executed with a competence that had once impressed him and now somehow irritated him. The candles she'd lit seemed accusatory in their romantic intent, casting shadows that highlighted the distance between them despite the intimate setting.

The silence stretched uncomfortably as they ate, punctuated only by the soft scrape of cutlery against porcelain and the distant hum of traffic seventeen floors below. Their penthouse had been Jennifer's idea, chosen for its view of the lake and its proximity to her law firm. John had preferred something closer to the airport, but he'd learned early in their marriage that Jennifer's preferences usually prevailed through sheer force of will and superior argumentation skills.

Jennifer set down her fork with deliberate precision, the slight sound echoing in the sudden silence. She was beautiful in the way that certain women were—commanding attention without seeking it, her presence filling rooms before she spoke a word.

At thirty-eight, she possessed the kind of refined elegance that came from good breeding, expensive education, and the confidence of someone who'd never doubted their place in the world. Her blonde hair was pulled back in a style that framed her angular face perfectly, and her green eyes held an intelligence that had initially captivated him and now often made him feel inadequate.

"John, we need to talk."

The words every married man dreaded, delivered with the professional tone she used in depositions. He looked up from his plate, wariness settling in his stomach like stones. This wasn't going to be about vacation plans or whose turn it was to call the cleaning service.

"What do I have to apologize for now?"

The defensiveness in his voice was automatic, honed by months of similar conversations that began with her dissatisfaction and ended with his promises to change behaviors he didn't fully understand were problematic.

"Can you tone down your sarcasm for a moment? We need to have a serious conversation about us."

The word 'us' hung between them, heavy with implications he wasn't prepared to examine. John's defensive walls rose automatically, constructed over years of feeling perpetually insufficient in the face of Jennifer's success, her social ease, her ability to navigate complex emotional terrain while he fumbled for the right words.

"What about us? We've been through this before. Our marriage is strong. We will survive this."

He'd said those exact words before, during previous iterations of this conversation. They'd become a mantra, repeated with diminishing conviction each time. But admitting weakness felt like surrendering ground in a battle he didn't understand he was fighting.

"No, John, you give us too much credit. Our marriage is not strong, and I don't know about you, but I know I can't keep pretending everything's okay."

Her words cut deeper than he expected, slicing through his careful denial with surgical precision. Jennifer never spoke carelessly; every word was chosen for maximum impact. When she said their marriage wasn't strong, she meant it had already failed in ways he was still too stubborn or blind to acknowledge.

John pushed his chair back slightly, creating physical distance from truths he wasn't ready to hear. The gesture was unconscious but telling—his body retreating even as his mind scrambled for counterarguments.

"I'm sorry I haven't been spending much time with you. My workload has been crazy lately. You know that."

It was true, technically. The airline had been short-staffed, and John had volunteered for extra flights, partly due to financial necessity and partly out of a desire to avoid the growing tension at home. Flying felt simple compared to marriage—clear procedures, predictable outcomes, problems that could be solved with checklists and experience rather than emotional intelligence he'd never developed.

Jennifer's laugh was bitter, devoid of humor. The sound was like breaking glass, sharp and final.

"It's not just work, John. It's more than that. We are growing apart."

The words he'd been dreading, delivered with the kind of calm finality that suggested she'd been thinking about this for months. How long had she been cataloging his failures, building her case like the litigator she was? How many times had he missed the signs, dismissed her concerns, chosen the easy path of avoidance over the difficult work of connection?

"When was the last time we talked about something that mattered?" she continued, her voice growing stronger as she warmed to her argument. "Talked, not just logistics, about bills and schedules, and whose family we're visiting for the holidays. When was the last time you asked me about my work, my dreams, anything beyond the surface?"

John felt trapped by the question because he couldn't remember. Their conversations had become functional, transactional exchanges of necessary information. He knew she'd made partner last year, that she was working on a high-profile corporate merger, but the details escaped him. When had he stopped caring about the things that animated her?

"I ask about your work all the time," he protested, though even as he said it, he knew it wasn't true.

"You ask if I had a good day. That's not the same thing." Jennifer's voice carried the frustration of someone who'd been trying to connect with a wall. "I tell you about winning cases, about the politics at my firm, about the young associates I'm mentoring, and you nod and say 'that's nice' and change the subject to something about flying or sports or anything that doesn't require you to engage with my life."

The accusation stung because it was accurate. John had perfected the art of appearing to listen while his mind wandered to flight schedules, mechanical issues, anything more concrete than the emotional complexities Jennifer navigated daily. Her world of legal strategy and office politics felt foreign to him, as incomprehensible as his world of aviation probably seemed to her.

"It's not just the conversations," she pressed on, her composure beginning to crack slightly. "It's the intimacy, John.

When was the last time you touched me without it being a prelude to sex? When was the last time we just held each other, or you ran your fingers through my hair while we watched a movie, or any of the small gestures that made me feel loved instead of just desired?"

The question hit him like turbulence—unexpected and disorienting. He could remember when those gestures had felt natural. Still, somewhere along the way, they'd been replaced by routine, by the kind of mechanical affection that kept marriages functioning without making them thrive.

Instead of engaging with her pain, John stood and pressed his lips to her forehead—a gesture that once meant comfort but now felt like dismissal, another way of avoiding the difficult conversation she was trying to have.

"You're too dramatic for me right now… I'm going to brush my teeth, take a shower, and meet you in bed."

The annoyance that flashed across Jennifer's face was instant and unmistakable. Still, John was already walking away, choosing avoidance over confrontation with the practiced ease of a man who'd perfected the art of emotional retreat. He heard her sharp intake of breath behind him, the sound of her chair scraping against the hardwood floor, but he didn't turn back.

In the bathroom, John avoided his own eyes in the mirror as he brushed his teeth with mechanical precision. The routine was soothing—something he could control and complete successfully, unlike the conversation he'd just abandoned. The hot water in the shower felt like absolution, washing away the day's tensions along with Jennifer's accusations.

But when he emerged, towel wrapped around his waist, he found her sitting on the edge of their king-sized bed, still fully dressed, her hands folded in her lap like a verdict waiting to be delivered.

"We're not done talking," she said quietly.

"Jen, I'm tired. Can we do this tomorrow?"

"No, John. We can't keep postponing this. I've been patient, I've tried to give you space to figure things out, but I can't pretend anymore that we're just going through a rough patch."

He sat beside her on the bed, the mattress dipping under his weight, and for a moment, the physical proximity felt like progress. But when he reached for her hand, she pulled away— a small rejection that felt enormous in the darkness.

"I love you," he said, the words feeling inadequate even as he spoke them.

"I know you do. But love isn't enough anymore, John. We need more than love to make this work. We need connection, communication, and effort. And I feel like I'm the only one trying."

Her voice broke slightly on the last word, and John felt a stab of guilt so sharp it took his breath away. When had he stopped trying? When had their marriage become something he endured rather than nurtured?

"What do you want from me?" he asked, and immediately regretted the phrasing. It sounded like an accusation rather than a genuine question.

"I want you to fight for us. I want you to care enough to have difficult conversations, rather than walking away. I want you to see me, really see me, not just the woman who happens to share your bed and your last name."

Later, in the darkness of their bedroom, he lay staring at the shadows on the ceiling while Jennifer pretended to sleep beside him. Her breathing was too controlled, too measured for genuine unconsciousness. The space between them on the king-sized mattress felt like an ocean, unbridgeable and cold.

He'd tried twice to initiate what they'd once playfully called "sexy time"—their code for intimacy that had gradually become more code than intimacy. The phrase had started as a joke years ago, a way to navigate desire with humor and affection. Now it felt juvenile, a relic of a marriage that had been younger and more hopeful.

Both attempts met with stone-still resistance, her body unresponsive as marble. She didn't push him away or say no— that would have required acknowledgment of his desire. Instead, she simply didn't respond, becoming absent even while physically present. The rejection was more devastating for its passivity; a withdrawal so complete it left him feeling like he was trying to make love to a stranger.

Deflated and frustrated, John rolled away from his wife and reached for his phone, which lit up with incoming messages. The blue glow illuminated his face in the darkness, and he angled the screen away from Jennifer's still form. The name on the display made his pulse quicken with guilt and anticipation: "MELISSA" in bold letters, each character a minor betrayal waiting to unfold.

I can't stop thinking about you, too, my love.

I miss you. When can we see each other again?

His thumbs hovered over the keyboard, caught between desire and conscience. Three weeks ago, Melissa had been just another flight attendant—competent, friendly, the kind of professional colleague he interacted with dozens of times without a second thought. But something had shifted during a layover in Denver, a conversation that had started about work and drifted into personal territory with dangerous ease.

She was twenty-eight, divorced, with the kind of uncomplicated warmth that Jennifer had once possessed but had gradually replaced with sophisticated coolness. Melissa laughed easily, touched his arm when she talked, and looked at him like he was interesting rather than inadequate. When she'd suggested drinks after their shift, John had told himself it was harmless collegiality.

The hotel bar had been dimly lit, filled with other airline crew members decompressing from their flights. Melissa had chosen a booth in the corner, sliding in beside him instead of across from him, her thigh warm against his. She smelled like vanilla and possibility, and when she leaned close to talk over the background noise, her breath tickled his ear in ways that reminded him he was still a man with desires and needs.

"You seem sad," she'd observed, her fingers tracing patterns on the condensation of her wine glass. "Married guys always seem a little sad."

John had protested that he wasn't sad, that his marriage was fine, but the words felt hollow even to him. Melissa had simply smiled and ordered another round. Somehow, the conversation had turned to all the ways his life had narrowed, all the dreams he'd deferred, all the parts of himself he'd buried under the weight of responsibility and routine.

When she'd kissed him in the elevator, soft and tentative and tasting like wine and rebellion, John had felt something awaken that he'd thought was permanently dormant. Not just desire—he could have resisted simple lust—but the intoxicating sensation of being wanted, truly wanted, by someone who saw him as he wished to be rather than as he feared he was.

They hadn't slept together that night. John had pulled away at the last moment, some vestige of honor or cowardice stopping him at the threshold of full betrayal. But they'd exchanged numbers, started texting, and begun the slow dance of an affair that felt inevitable even as it horrified him.

Soon. I promise.

His thumbs moved across the screen with practiced efficiency, typing words that felt more honest than anything he'd said to Jennifer in months. The irony wasn't lost on him— he could be authentic with a woman he barely knew while growing increasingly distant from the woman he'd promised to love and honor until death.

The phone buzzed again almost immediately.

I had a dream about you last night. We were flying together, just the two of us, somewhere tropical and beautiful: no schedules, no responsibilities, just us and the sky.

John closed his eyes, allowing himself to sink into the fantasy. No marriage is slowly dying through neglect and mutual resentment.

No conversations about feelings and needs, and all the ways he'd failed to be the husband Jennifer deserved. Just the simple pleasure of being appreciated, desired, and seen as someone worthy of dreams and longing.

That sounds perfect.

I know you feel guilty, but John... you deserve to be happy. You deserve to be with someone who appreciates you.

The words were seductive precisely because they offered absolution along with desire. Melissa wasn't just offering sex—she was offering a narrative in which he was the wounded party, the misunderstood hero rather than the failing husband. It was a story that transformed his selfishness into self-preservation, his betrayal into an act of courage.

Beside him, Jennifer shifted in her sleep, murmuring something unintelligible. In the blue glow of his phone, her face looked younger, more vulnerable, stripped of the professional armor she wore during their waking conflicts. This was the woman he'd fallen in love with—brilliant, beautiful, fierce in her convictions but soft in her private moments.

For a moment, guilt overwhelmed desire. What was he doing? How had he allowed himself to drift so far from the man he'd once been, the man who'd stood at an altar and meant every word of his vows? But then Jennifer's face hardened even in sleep, her jaw clenching with the stress she carried even into unconsciousness, and the moment of connection dissolved.

His phone buzzed again.

I'm working the Portland route next week. Layover Tuesday night. Please say you'll be there.

Portland. He wasn't scheduled for that route, but trades could be arranged, shifts could be swapped. All it would take was a few phone calls, some manipulation of the scheduling system he knew inside and out.

I'll make it work.

I can't wait to see you. To hold you. To show you how a man like you should be treated.

John set his phone aside and stared at the ceiling, his heart racing with anticipation and self-loathing in equal measure. Somewhere in the darkness beside him, his marriage was dying with the slow, inevitable progression of a terminal illness. And instead of fighting for it, instead of being the man Jennifer needed him to be, he was planning his next betrayal.

The apartment that had once felt warm now seemed like a beautiful prison, filled with photographs of people they used to be and promises they could no longer keep. In the morning, they would resume their careful dance of avoidance and recrimination, and John would continue his slow transformation from faithful husband to adulterous stranger.

But tonight, in the darkness, he allowed himself to dream of Portland, of hotel rooms and possibilities, of a woman who saw him not as he was but as he wished to be. It was a small comfort and a large betrayal, but it was all he had left to sustain him through the wreckage of his marriage and the growing certainty that some things, once broken, could never be repaired.

The office building buzzed with its usual morning energy when John arrived the next day, the familiar symphony of ringing phones, clicking keyboards, and muffled conversations creating a backdrop of professional normalcy that felt increasingly foreign to his fractured state of mind. The airline's headquarters occupied three floors of the downtown tower, its sterile corporate aesthetics—beige walls, fluorescent lighting, motivational posters about teamwork and safety were designed to inspire confidence and efficiency rather than comfort.

John's desk sat in the middle of the pilot scheduling office, surrounded by the organized chaos of flight rosters, weather reports, and maintenance bulletins that kept the airline's operations running smoothly. Usually, he found solace in this environment, in the predictable rhythms of aviation bureaucracy that felt manageable compared to the emotional turbulence of his personal life. But today, even this sanctuary felt compromised.

He'd barely settled at his desk, computer still booting up and coffee growing cold in his company-issued mug, when Tom materialized in his doorway like a bad omen made flesh. Captain Thomas Reeves carried himself with the kind of swagger that made John's teeth ache—shoulders back, chin raised, every gesture broadcasting a confidence that seemed inversely proportional to his actual competence.

At thirty-nine, Tom was younger than John by just four years, but possessed the kind of political savvy that had fasttracked him through the ranks despite, or perhaps because of, his tendency to cut corners when he thought no one was watching.

"Morning, John."

The greeting was casual, almost friendly, but John had learned to listen for the undercurrents in Tom's voice. There was always something else lurking beneath his words— calculation, manipulation, the constant assessment of advantage and weakness that made every interaction feel like a chess match played with loaded dice.

"Morning, Tom."

John's response was carefully neutral, a diplomatic nonengagement that he'd perfected over months of increasingly uncomfortable encounters. He kept his eyes on his computer screen, hoping to project the kind of busy professionalism that might discourage extended conversation. The quarterly safety reports needed reviewing, and he'd been putting off the tedious work of updating his flight log entries— tasks that suddenly seemed urgent compared to whatever Tom wanted to discuss.

"How're you and your beautiful wife, Jenn, holding up? It looked crazy the way you two were yelling at each other that day at my barbecue event."

The casual observation hit like a calculated blow; each word precisely chosen for maximum impact. John's fingers froze over his keyboard as the memory rushed back with nauseating clarity—Tom's Fourth of July barbecue three months ago, the kind of mandatory social gathering that airline employees attended to maintain the illusion of collegial friendship.

Jennifer had been on edge all day, her lawyer's instincts picking up on undercurrents that John had either missed or chosen to ignore.

The argument had started over something trivial—John's third beer before noon, or maybe his failure to engage with the spouses' conversation about local politics. But it had escalated quickly, their voices rising above the background noise of children playing and meat sizzling on the grill. Other guests had pretended not to notice, engaging in elaborate performances of distraction while John and Jennifer's marriage imploded in real-time.

"She's perfectly fine talking to other people, but the minute I try to contribute to the conversation, I'm wrong about everything," Jennifer had hissed, her voice low but venomous. "You make me look like an idiot in front of your colleagues."

"I was just trying to lighten the mood," John had protested, aware that other conversations had grown quieter around them. "You were getting worked up about something that doesn't even affect us."

"Everything affects us, John. That's what you don't understand. We're a team, or at least we're supposed to be, but you act like my opinions don't matter unless they align perfectly with yours."

The memory of Tom watching them from across the patio, his expression unreadable but attentive, made John's stomach churn with retrospective embarrassment. How long had he been observing? What conclusions had he drawn from their public dysfunction? And most importantly, why was he bringing it up now?

John's smile faltered as he processed the implications— Tom had been watching them, cataloging their dysfunction for future reference.

The realization felt like a violation, as if his private pain had become public entertainment for someone who had no business witnessing it, much less commenting on it.

"She's fine. We're fine. Husband and wife sometimes argue, but I understand where you're coming from. And um… I appreciate your advice."

The words came out more defensive than John intended, each syllable betraying the very weakness he was trying to conceal. He could hear the strain in his voice, the forced casualness that fooled no one, least of all someone like Tom who had made a career of reading people's vulnerabilities and exploiting them.

What advice had Tom given? John struggled to remember any specific guidance from that day, any words of wisdom or support that might justify his grateful response. The truth was more complicated and infinitely more disturbing—Tom's "advice" had been a series of observations and suggestions that felt more like reconnaissance than friendship.

"Marriage is hard work," Tom had said, appearing at John's elbow with fresh beers and the knowing smile that suggested intimate familiarity with marital dysfunction. "Sometimes people grow apart, you know? Different interests, different priorities. The key is figuring out whether you're growing in the same direction or just growing apart."

At the time, the words had felt supportive, even insightful. Tom had shared his own divorce story with apparent candor—how his ex-wife had accused him of emotional unavailability, how they'd tried counseling but ultimately decided they wanted different things from life. It had felt like a sense of solidarity, one struggling husband to another.

But now, weeks later and with his marriage officially dissolved, John wondered if Tom's concern had been genuine or strategic. Had he been offering support, or had he been planting seeds of doubt? The distinction mattered more than John wanted to admit, because it would determine whether Tom was an ally or something far more dangerous.

Tom's smirk widened before he headed to his desk, the expression carrying layers of meaning that John couldn't quite decode. There was satisfaction there, certainly, but also something that looked almost like anticipation. He moved with the casual confidence of someone who believed he held all the cards, his stride purposeful as he navigated between the maze of cubicles and offices that made up their shared workspace.

John watched as he settled into his chair. Tom's desk was positioned diagonally across the office, close enough for casual conversation but far enough away to maintain the illusion of privacy. From his vantage point, John could observe without seeming to stare, a skill he'd developed over months of growing unease about his colleague's motives and methods.

Suspicion gnawed at John's consciousness like a persistent ache, the kind of nagging doubt that colored every interaction and cast shadows over the most innocent exchanges. It was an uncomfortable feeling, this certainty that something was wrong coupled with the complete inability to identify what, exactly, was causing his alarm. Tom had never done anything overtly threatening or inappropriate—his transgressions were subtle, cumulative, the kind of boundary violations that were difficult to report because they lived in the spaces between official policies and human decency.

But John lacked the evidence to justify his growing unease. What could he report? Does Tom ask too many personal questions? Does his concern feel performative rather than genuine? Was his presence at social gatherings seemed calculated rather than coincidental? These were impressions, instincts, the kind of gut feelings that had served John well in the cockpit but carried little weight in corporate environments that valued documentation over intuition.

The morning wore on with excruciating normalcy. John attempted to focus on his work—reviewing flight schedules, updating training certifications, responding to emails from crew coordinators—but his attention kept drifting to Tom's desk. His colleague appeared to be working diligently, his phone pressed to his ear as he discussed route changes with dispatch, his fingers flying over the keyboard as he updated flight logs. To any casual observer, Tom appeared to be the epitome of professional competence.

But John noticed things others might miss. The way Tom's conversations grew quieter when specific names were mentioned. His computer screen always seemed to be angled away from passing colleagues. The carefully casual way he asked about other pilots' schedules, their personal lives, and their relationships. It could all be innocent professional curiosity, the kind of water-cooler conversation that lubricated workplace relationships. Or it could be something else entirely.

Around ten-thirty, Tom's phone rang with a call that made him sit up straight in his chair, his usual casual demeanor shifting into something more focused and intense. John couldn't hear the conversation, but he could read body language well enough to recognize the signs of someone receiving important information. Tom took notes, asked clarifying questions, and ended the call with what appeared to be satisfaction.

Within minutes, Tom was at John's desk again, this time without the casual friendliness of their earlier encounter. "Hey, John. Got a minute? There's something we need to discuss."

The shift in tone was subtle but unmistakable. Gone was the smirking confidence, replaced by something that felt almost official. John's chest tightened with the familiar sensation of impending conflict, the way his body had learned to prepare for turbulence before his conscious mind recognized the signs.

"What's on your mind?"

"Let's grab some privacy. Conference room two is empty."

The suggestion felt less like a request than a command, and John found himself following Tom down the hallway toward the small conference room they used for sensitive discussions. The room was austere, with white walls, a circular table surrounded by six chairs, and a whiteboard that still bore traces of equations from the previous week's safety meeting. Tom closed the door behind them with deliberate precision, the soft click of the latch somehow ominous in the confined space.

"I've been hearing some things," Tom began, settling into a chair across from John with the kind of careful positioning that suggested this conversation had been planned rather than impromptu. "Concerns about your recent performance,

questions about your... stability."

The words hung in the air like an accusation waiting to be substantiated. John felt his face flush with a mixture of anger and embarrassment, but he forced himself to remain seated, to project calm despite the chaos erupting in his chest.

"What kind of concerns? From who?"

"Does it matter? The point is, people are starting to notice things. Your distraction during briefings, the way you've been isolating yourself from the crew, the obvious stress you've been under since those overwhelming frictions with your wife been increasing."

Each observation felt like a small, precise, and poisonous knife thrust. The worst part was that Tom wasn't wrong— John had been distracted, isolated, struggling to maintain his professional composure while his personal life imploded. But hearing these private struggles catalogued with such clinical detachment felt like a betrayal of trust he'd never explicitly given.

"I'm dealing with some personal issues, but they haven't affected my flying. My safety record is impeccable, and you know it."

"I do know it, which is why I'm trying to help you here, John. But perception matters in this business. If people start questioning your judgment, your competence, it doesn't matter how good your record is. They'll find reasons to ground you, to question your fitness for duty."

The threat was delivered with the kind of false concern that made John's skin crawl. Tom was positioning himself as an ally while simultaneously outlining the ways John's career could be destroyed, creating a narrative in which he was both the problem and the solution.

"What exactly are you suggesting?"

Tom leaned forward, his expression shifting into something that might have been sincere if John hadn't learned to distrust everything about him.

"I'm suggesting you need someone in your corner— someone who understands the system, who knows how to manage perceptions and protect careers. I'm offering to be that person, John. To help you navigate this difficult period and come out stronger on the other side."

The offer was seductive in its simplicity—protection in exchange for... what, exactly? Tom hadn't specified his terms, but John understood enough about power dynamics to recognize a shakedown when he heard one. The question was what Tom wanted in return for his "help," and whether John could afford to refuse.

"I appreciate the offer," John said carefully, "but I think I can handle my career."

Tom's smile was patient, almost pitying. "Of course you can. But why make it harder than it needs to be? Why fight battles you don't have to fight when you could have an ally instead of an enemy?"

The words carried an unmistakable implication—that Tom could be either an ally or enemy, depending on John's response to this carefully orchestrated conversation. It was extortion disguised as friendship, a protection racket operating within the sterile confines of corporate aviation.

John stood, his chair scraping against the floor with a sound that seemed unnaturally loud in the small room. "I need to get back to work."

"Think about what I said," Tom called after him as John reached for the door handle. "The offer stands, but it won't stand forever. People are watching, John. Make sure you're on the right side when they make their decision."

Walking back to his desk, John felt the weight of every stare, real or imagined. His colleagues continued their work with apparent indifference, but he couldn't shake the feeling that Tom's web of observation and manipulation extended far beyond their interactions. How many conversations had been reported back to him? How many casual observations had been transformed into evidence of John's alleged instability?

The paranoia was exhausting, but John couldn't entirely dismiss it. In an industry where safety was paramount and public trust was everything, even the suggestion of impairment could be career-ending. Tom understood this better than most, and he was prepared to use that knowledge as a form of leverage.

Settling back into his chair, John tried to focus on the mundane tasks that filled his days—schedule reviews, training updates, the endless paperwork that kept commercial aviation running smoothly. But concentration felt impossible with Tom's implicit threats echoing in his mind. The office that had once felt like neutral territory now seemed hostile; every interaction potentially compromised by ulterior motives he couldn't fully understand.

His computer screen showed seventeen new emails, including one from the chief pilot's office requesting updated fitness-for-duty documentation. The timing felt suspicious, coming so soon after Tom's veiled warnings about perception and performance. Was this routine administrative maintenance, or was someone already building a case for his removal?

John's hands trembled slightly as he reached for his coffee, the minor betrayal of nerves visible to anyone who might be watching. He forced his fingers to steady, schooled his expression into professional neutrality, and began the careful work of protecting himself from an enemy who wore the mask of a friend.

The morning stretched ahead with ominous uncertainty, each moment pregnant with the possibility of further revelation or attack. Tom had shown his hand just enough to reveal his willingness to weaponize personal information, but not sufficient to expose the full scope of his intentions. It was a masterful display of psychological warfare, leaving John to wonder how long he'd been fighting a battle he didn't even know had begun.

The company party arrived three weeks later, complete with all the forced merriment that corporate events demand. John nursed a glass of wine while making obligatory small talk with colleagues, his attention repeatedly drawn to Jennifer's location across the room. She stood too close to Tom, their interaction carrying an intimacy that made John's chest tighten with a sense of recognition.

Captain Adam appeared at his elbow, wine glass in hand, following John's gaze to where Tom was attempting to lick cake frosting from the corner of Jennifer's mouth. She giggled like a schoolgirl, encouraging his advance with body language that screamed availability.

"Seems like your relationship is going worse than I thought. Don't go over there and get angry at Tom. He's not married to you. If you're going to get upset, you better get upset at your wife."

John drained his wine in one burning gulp and handed the empty glass back to Captain Adam. The alcohol provided false courage as he crossed the room, his footsteps measured and deliberate.

"Jenn… I guess we need to talk?"

Tom stepped back, sensing the shift in atmospheric pressure that preceded emotional storms. Jennifer followed John to a quieter corner, her earlier playfulness evaporating into irritation.

"What is it now, John? 'Cause God forbid if I needed to talk, all you would do is go to sleep. But the king needs to talk. So, the world must stop and attend to his needs."

Her sarcasm was a weapon they'd both sharpened over months of accumulated resentment. John kept his voice low, a dangerous tone.

"I've known Tom for seven years now. Never did I ever see anyone laugh at all his jokes while caressing his arm… care to explain yourself?"

"Explain what? Last I checked, you're not my father. I'm not your kid; I'm your wife, and I'm allowed to have male friends.

I'm so sorry 'cause evil thinks what evil does. and Tom… We're just talking."

"Talking? The man trying to lick crumbs off the side of your face is just talking? Or the way your hands were all over him. Is that a more accurate description of 'just talking'?"

Jennifer rolled her eyes with theatrical exaggeration and walked away, leaving John standing alone with his suspicions and growing rage.

"I knew I should not have come to your stupid corporate party. I need some air."

John waited in their apartment until nearly midnight, pacing between the kitchen and living room like a caged animal. When Jennifer finally returned, her disheveled appearance and guilty expression told the story her words would soon confirm.

"Somebody had a good night, care to share? I know Tom looked angry at the party when you left. I'm guessing he's not anymore."

"I'm tired, I'm not in the mood to talk right now. We'll talk in the morning."

But John was done with delays and deflections. He slipped his wedding ring from his finger and placed it on the table between them with deliberate ceremony.

"Well, you're going to have to talk to me right now. You left the party claiming you needed air. I'm not stupid, so how long has this thing between you and Tom been going?"

The question hung in the air like smoke from a fire that had been smoldering for months. Jennifer's composure cracked, revealing the raw truth beneath the facade.

"You finally notice me? Yes, I slept with Tom. But all I wanted to do was try to get you to work on our marriage. Can't you see we've been growing apart?"

John stepped closer, his face inches from hers, his voice dropping to a whisper that carried more menace than shouting ever could.

"We've been growing apart, I get that. So, how does sleeping with Tom bring us back together?"

The color drained from Jennifer's cheeks as the absurdity of her logic became apparent even to her.

"All I wanted was for you to notice me… make you see I matter too, I got tired waiting for you to come home. Tom was just a mistake."

"A mistake? How long, Jennifer? How long have you been making 'mistakes' with Tom?"

Her voice trembled as she spoke, each word a small confession extracted under pressure.

"Okay, that's a fair question. And you deserve to know the truth. It's been six months, but I promise you I'm going to change. I'm going back to be the wife you first fell in love with."

John's laugh was harsh and bitter, the sound of something precious being torn apart.

"Six months. Wow… That's funny… that's the same amount of time I've been seeing Melissa."

Jennifer's eyes widened with shock and hurt, her mouth opening and closing without sound.

"Melissa? Who the hell is Melissa??? Can you repeat what you just said?"

"Yes, Jennifer. You're not the only one who enjoys playing games. I want a divorce."

The luxury hotel lobby gleamed with marble and crystal, its opulence a stark contrast to the emptiness John carried inside. He moved through the space with determined steps, pressing the elevator button with more force than necessary. The hallway stretched before him like a runway, and he navigated it with the same precision he used to land aircraft in crosswinds.

Melissa was waiting when he opened the door—late twenty-something, beautiful in the way that made men forget their responsibilities. Before she could speak, John grabbed her with desperate hunger, months of frustration and betrayal channeling into pure physical need.

Their encounter was rough, passionate, and entirely consensual—she met his intensity with her own, encouraging him with words and sounds that made him feel decades younger. When they finally collapsed together an hour later, the hotel room bore the evidence of their collision: scattered clothes, tangled sheets, and the lingering scent of desire fulfilled.

"What got into you? You miss me that much? You was like a man possessed," Melissa whispered against his chest.

"I'm done with Jennifer; I filed for divorce."

The words carried finality that surprised him with their clarity. Melissa lifted her head, studying his face in the dim light filtering through hotel curtains.

"Baby, are you okay… What are you thinking about?"

John's expression was complex—part relief, part guilt, part something darker he couldn't name.

"Can you believe she was cheating as well?"

Melissa arranged her features into surprised concern, though John suspected she'd been waiting for this moment since their affair began.

"She doesn't deserve you, baby. I would never take you for granted. I love you so much. You are so giving… so caring. I will always put you first in my life."

He studied her face, seeing her clearly for perhaps the first time—beautiful, young, expensive to maintain. Like a Ferrari that ordinary people rented for special occasions, but never bought because the maintenance costs would bankrupt them.

"You love me?"

"Yes, I do… we do have something real. Don't we?"

John wanted to say so much more, but the words would have sounded crueler than he was prepared to be. Instead, he kissed her, letting the gesture speak for thoughts he couldn't voice.

"We do."

But even as he said it, John wondered if anything in his life was real anymore, or if he was simply trading one illusion for another, one mistake for the next, in an endless cycle of choices that led nowhere but deeper into the darkness he'd been running from all along.

CHAPTER 2
COLLISION COURSE

Dawn crept through the apartment windows like an unwelcome intruder, casting pale light across surfaces John had hoped would remain hidden in darkness. He slipped his key into the lock with surgical precision, each movement calculated to avoid the telltale sounds of a man returning from somewhere he shouldn't have been. The silence stretched between his footsteps and his conscience, heavy with the weight of choices made in hotel rooms and lies told in marriage beds.

But Jennifer was already awake.

She sat on their couch—their couch, not his couch, though the distinction felt meaningless now—with her legs tucked beneath her like a wounded animal seeking shelter. Her eyes bore the red-rimmed evidence of tears shed in solitude, and the sight of her struck him with unexpected force. She was still his wife, still the woman who'd once laughed at his terrible jokes.

There had been a time when she didn't need to ask where he was.

She would just lean into him, her head finding his shoulder like it belonged there, her body settling without hesitation. The quiet hum of the cabin would wrap around them, soft and constant, while the world outside disappeared into darkness.

He used to feel her breathe. Slow. Even. Certain.

Sometimes she would shift slightly, adjusting closer, like she was making sure he was still there. And he always was.

Back then, silence didn't feel heavy.

It felt... shared. "Where have you been?"

The question hung between them like smoke from a house fire—simple words that carried the weight of their entire relationship. Her voice held winter in every syllable, cold and unforgiving.

John's mouth opened and closed, words scrambling in his throat like frightened birds. "I think that question should be directed to Tom, not me."

The deflection was weak, and they both recognized it. Jennifer's composure cracked, revealing the raw anger beneath her grief.

"I stopped seeing Tom… please use a different excuse 'cause it's been four months now… John, please… we can still save our marriage?"

The desperation in her voice was a knife twisting in wounds he'd convinced himself had healed. John remained silent, his lack of response confirming what they both already understood—some damage cut too deep for bandages and apologies.

Jennifer rose from the couch with the unsteady grace of someone who'd forgotten how to move through their own life. Her face cycled through betrayal, anger, and something approaching panic.

"Baby, look at me. We have history together. Please don't throw it all away."

History. The word echoed in the space between them, carrying the weight of shared anniversaries, whispered promises, and dreams they'd built together before tearing them down with their own hands. John exhaled slowly, the sound carrying finality he hadn't intended to voice.

"I told you already I don't want to stay in this marriage."

"We both cheated, and I get it, two wrongs don't make a right, but baby, please, I'm willing to move past this… why can't you?"

Her scream split the morning quiet, raw and desperate. John winced at the sound, at the way her voice broke on the word 'please.' He'd heard that same break in passengers' voices during emergency situations—the moment when hope transformed into understanding.

When he spoke, his voice carried the quiet authority he'd perfected in cockpits during storms.

"I only have sex for fun. You were having sex with my coworker to spite me. It's really not the same level of infidelity. If I stay with you, I will have to punch Tom in the face. So that means I would lose my job… you're not worth it."

The words landed like blows; each one precisely calibrated to wound. Jennifer's face transformed, the last traces of pleading evaporating into something harder, more resolved.

She grabbed her coat with movements sharp enough to cut glass. "I guess there's nothing left for us to talk about."

The door closed behind her with surprising gentleness, as if even the apartment itself had grown tired of their dramatic exits.

Three weeks later…

The courthouse steps stretched before them like a ceremonial staircase leading to nowhere, each granite slab worn smooth by decades of people ascending toward justice or descending into defeat. John emerged into the afternoon sunlight, which felt too bright for the occasion, squinting against the harsh glare that seemed to mock the darkness of his mood. The October air carried the crisp promise of winter, but he felt only the hollow emptiness that followed the completion of something that should never have needed completing.

His lawyer's voice faded into background noise as final details dissolved into legal jargon and filing fees—words like "irreconcilable differences" and "equitable distribution" that reduced seven years of marriage to a series of financial calculations and custody arrangements that didn't apply to them. Richard Chambers was a competent divorce attorney, recommended by a colleague who'd walked this same path two years earlier, but his clinical approach to marital dissolution made John feel like a case file rather than a human being experiencing the systematic dismantling of his adult life.

"The decree will be final in thirty days," Richard was saying, his voice carrying the practiced efficiency of someone who'd delivered this speech hundreds of times. "You'll receive copies of all filed documents within this week. Remember, the asset division we negotiated is binding, so make sure you transfer the investment account funds by the fifteenth of next month."

Jennifer stood twenty feet away, surrounded by her support system—her sister Rachel, whose disapproval of John had been evident from their first meeting; her best friend from law school, a woman whose name John had never learned but whose hostile stares he'd endured at countless social gatherings; and her own attorney, Miranda Walsh, whose reputation for aggressive representation had been both intimidating and, John had to admit, impressive to witness in action.

The contrast between their respective entourages was stark and telling. John had Richard and no one else, while Jennifer was flanked by people who'd obviously been preparing for this day with the kind of strategic planning that had made her such a formidable litigator. They spoke in hushed tones, their body language radiating the solidarity of people who'd witnessed domestic dysfunction and chosen sides accordingly.

Jennifer's posture spoke to a resolution he both envied and resented. She stood with her shoulders back; chin raised in the confident stance that had first attracted him at a bar association mixer nine years ago. Her navy suit was perfectly tailored, her hair styled with the kind of professional polish that had become her armor against vulnerability. She looked like someone who'd emerged victorious from a difficult battle, while John felt like collateral damage from a war, he'd never fully understood he was fighting.

The irony wasn't lost on him that they were ending their marriage on the same courthouse steps where they'd obtained their marriage license close to a decade earlier. He could remember that day with painful clarity—how they'd laughed about the bureaucratic romance of government paperwork, how Jennifer had kissed him in the parking lot while joking about making their relationship "legally binding." The optimism of that moment felt like it belonged to different people, strangers who'd borrowed their faces and voices for a brief, shining performance of love and possibility.

Their eyes met once across the courthouse plaza—a moment that stretched longer than it should have, filled with words neither would speak. In her gaze, John saw flashes of the woman he'd fallen in love with —the brilliant attorney who had challenged him intellectually and supported him emotionally during the early years of his career advancement. But he also saw the disappointment that had gradually replaced affection, the way she'd learned to look at him like a problem to be solved rather than a partner to be cherished.

For a heartbeat, he wondered if she was remembering better times too—their honeymoon in Greece, lazy Sunday mornings reading newspapers in bed, the way she used to steal his pilot's cap and wear it while making breakfast, claiming it gave her "authority over aviation cuisine." But then her expression hardened, professional distance reasserting itself like a door closing on a room he'd never enter again. The sevenyear itch is really a thing.

She turned away first, stepping into a waiting car that carried her toward a future he wouldn't be part of. The black sedan—Miranda's vehicle, John realized—pulled away from the curb with quiet efficiency, taking with it the last tangible connection to the man he'd once been. He watched the vehicle disappear into downtown traffic, its taillights blinking like punctuation marks at the end of a sentence he'd never wanted to finish.

Richard clapped him on the shoulder with the kind of forced heartiness that lawyers used to mask their discomfort with clients' emotional responses. "These things are never easy, John, but you handled yourself well in there. Jennifer's team came prepared for a fight, but we held our ground. The settlement is fair, all things considered."

Fair. The word felt hollow in the context of dismantling a marriage. How did you fairly divide memories, shared dreams, the accumulated intimacy of two people who'd once believed they were building something permanent? The financial aspects had been straightforward enough—John kept the condo, Jennifer retained her partnership stake and retirement accounts, and they split the investment portfolio down the middle. But the emotional mathematics of divorce defied calculation.

"Thanks, Richard. I appreciate everything you did."

"Take care of yourself. And remember what we discussed about the asset transfers. Don't let them drag this out longer than necessary."

John nodded and walked toward his car, each step feeling heavier than the last. The parking garage was dim and cool, offering relief from the too-bright sunshine and the weight of curious stares from courthouse staff who'd witnessed his personal drama unfold in their professional space. His hands shook slightly as he fumbled with his keys, the small betrayal of nerves visible to anyone who might be watching.

The drive home passed in a blur of traffic lights and halfheard radio chatter. His mind wandered to the practical implications of his new status—changing emergency contacts on his pilot certification, updating insurance beneficiaries, and removing Jennifer's name from the dozens of accounts and services that had bound their lives together. The administrative aftermath of divorce was perhaps worse than the emotional trauma, reducing years of shared life to a series of phone calls and form modifications.

But instead of heading home to his empty condo and the mountain of paperwork waiting on his kitchen table, John found himself driving toward the airport. It was his day off, and he had no professional reason to be there, but the familiar route felt automatic, comforting in its predictability.

The airport bar had become his refuge during the worst months of his marriage's dissolution, the one place where his competence remained unquestioned and his identity felt solid.

Though Mike the bartender was neither priest nor therapist—simply a man who'd learned to read the stories written in the faces of travelers passing through. The establishment occupied a corner of Terminal B, strategically positioned to catch passengers with long layovers and airline employees seeking liquid comfort between shifts. It was neither elegant nor seedy; it was just a functional space that served its purpose with honest efficiency.

Mike was working the afternoon shift, as John had expected him to be. The bartender possessed the kind of reliable presence that frequent customers came to depend on—always there when needed, never intrusive but somehow available when conversation felt necessary. He was perhaps fifty, with graying hair and the kind of weathered face that suggested experience with life's complications. His approach to customer service was refreshingly straightforward: he served drinks competently and listened without judgment when people needed to talk.

John claimed his usual stool at the far end of the bar, away from the clusters of business travelers and airline staff who populated the middle sections. The positioning was strategic—close enough to signal availability for conversation but far enough to maintain privacy when solitude felt necessary. Mike approached with a knowing nod, already reaching for the bottle of bourbon that had become John's standard order.

"Captain John, don't tell me you got a flight today? You look like shit."

Mike's observation was delivered with the casual brutality of someone who'd seen too many men drowning in airport bars to bother with polite euphemisms. His directness was oddly comforting—no pretense, no careful tiptoeing around obvious truths, just honest assessment from someone who'd witnessed enough human wreckage to recognize the signs.

John managed a bitter chuckle as he accepted the glass Mike slid across the polished bar surface. "No, actually, it's my day off. I finalized my divorce papers. And I guess I forgot to shave."

The admission hung in the air between them, simple and devastating. John had told very few people about the divorce proceedings, preferring to maintain professional distance from colleagues who might view his personal failures as potential professional liabilities. But something about Mike's straightforward approach made confession feel safe, or at least manageable.

"Wanna talk about it?"

The invitation hung between them, simple and genuine. Mike's tone carried no curiosity or judgment, just the quiet offer of someone who'd heard countless stories and understood that sometimes speaking the truth aloud was the only way to begin processing it. John stared into his glass, watching the ice cubes melt like time-lapse footage of his marriage, each drop of dilution representing another compromise, another disappointment, another moment when love had proven insufficient to bridge the growing distance between two people who had once believed they were perfectly matched.

"There's really nothing to talk about. She cheated, I cheated, and now I'm regretting everything I did."

The words came out flatter than he'd intended, stripped of the emotional complexity that had made every day of the past eleven months feel like navigating through turbulence. Reducing their marriage's failure to a simple exchange of betrayals felt reductive and dishonest. Still, it was the only explanation that didn't require him to examine the deeper failures of character and commitment that had made infidelity seem like a reasonable response to marital unhappiness.

Mike nodded with the kind of understanding that didn't require elaboration. He'd probably heard variations of this story dozens of times—successful professionals who'd let their personal lives implode while maintaining their professional competence. These people could manage complex responsibilities but couldn't figure out how to love and be loved without destroying the very thing they'd claimed to cherish.

"That's tough, man. Sometimes things like this happen to give us a wake-up call."

The observation was offered without condescension, delivered in the matter-of-fact tone Mike typically used for his philosophical observations. He'd developed a reputation among regular customers for practical wisdom dispensed in small doses, insights that felt earned rather than borrowed from self-help books or motivational speakers.

John lifted his eyes from the amber liquid, meeting Mike's gaze with something approaching humor. "Interesting, well, I feel pretty awake now."

They shared a moment of understanding, two men who'd learned that consciousness wasn't always a blessing. Being awake meant confronting truths that sleep had temporarily obscured, acknowledging mistakes that couldn't be undone, and consequences that couldn't be avoided. John felt hyperaware of everything—the taste of bourbon on his tongue, the sound of conversations around him, the weight of his wedding ring that he'd finally removed that morning and placed in his dresser drawer like a piece of evidence from a crime scene.

"Another?" Mike asked, gesturing toward John's nearly empty glass.

John shook his head. "Better not. I still have to drive home and face the reality of being a divorced man."

"That's probably wise. But you know where to find me if you need to talk more."

The offer was genuine, carrying no expectation or obligation. Mike had perfected the art of being available without being pushy, present without being intrusive. It was a skill that probably developed over years of managing the emotional needs of travelers and airline employees who found themselves stranded between departure and arrival, suspended in the liminal space that airports occupy between one life and another.

John left cash on the bar—enough to cover his drinks and a generous tip that acknowledged Mike's informal counseling services—and walked back toward the parking garage. The airport was busy with its usual afternoon rhythm, passengers hurrying between gates while ground crews prepared aircraft for evening departures. The controlled chaos that had once energized him now felt overwhelming, too much stimulation for his current emotional state.

The drive home took longer than usual, traffic heavy with rush-hour commuters eager to escape their workdays and return to families and homes that presumably provided comfort rather than conflict. John envied their certainty of destination and their confidence in what awaited them at the end of their journeys. His own home felt foreign now, a space that had been designed for two people but would now house only one, a daily reminder of his failure to maintain the most important relationship of his adult life.

Later, in the darkness of his apartment, John lay staring at the shadows on the ceiling, his mind replaying the day's events with exhausting repetition. The condo felt different now that it was officially his alone—larger and smaller simultaneously, full of empty spaces where

Jennifer's presence had once provided warmth and companionship. Her books were gone from the shelves, her clothes absent from the closet, her toiletries no longer cluttering the bathroom counter. The absence was more noticeable than her presence had been toward the end, a vacuum that seemed to amplify every sound and shadow.

His phone buzzed with incoming messages, the blue glow illuminating his face in the darkness. Melissa's name appeared on the screen, her words glowing like accusations in the darkness:

Hey, thinking about you.

Hope you're okay.

I miss you.

The message carried layers of complexity that John wasn't prepared to navigate. Melissa represented the path he'd chosen when his marriage became unbearable, the temporary escape that had provided relief from domestic dysfunction while simultaneously contributing to it. Their affair had been both symptom and cause of his marital problems, a betrayal that had felt justified in the moment but seemed inexcusable in hindsight.

He read the message twice before placing the phone face down on his nightstand, closing his eyes against the weight of choices that had seemed so clear in hotel rooms but felt murky in the solitude of his own bed. The affair with Melissa had ended weeks ago, terminated by mutual agreement as his divorce proceedings intensified and his conscience finally overcame her desire. But their connection hadn't completely dissolved, leaving both of them in the uncomfortable position of caring about someone they couldn't be with and shouldn't want. Feeling guilty, he grabbed his phone and replied.

I'm okay.

Just need some time to figure things out.

He typed the response and immediately deleted it, then tried again:

Thanks for thinking of me. Today

was difficult, but I'm managing.

That felt too formal, too distant for someone who'd provided comfort during his darkest months. Finally, he settled on simplicity:

I'm okay.

Thanks for asking.

The response felt inadequate but honest, acknowledging her concern without encouraging further contact. Melissa deserved better than to be a placeholder for his unresolved guilt and confusion, just as Jennifer had deserved better than the distracted, defensive husband he'd become during their final years together.

John placed the phone back on his nightstand and stared at the ceiling, counting shadows and trying to identify the moment when his life had become so complicated. The man who'd stood at an altar almost eight years ago and promised to love, honor, and cherish Jennifer Morrison until death do us part had believed those words completely. That man had possessed confidence in his ability to build and maintain a marriage, to be the kind of husband who provided stability and partnership rather than disappointment and betrayal.

Somewhere along the way, that man had disappeared, replaced by someone who could rationalize infidelity and emotional unavailability as reasonable responses to marital difficulty. The transformation hadn't been sudden or dramatic—no single moment of moral collapse that could be identified and regretted. Instead, it had been gradual, a series of small compromises and justifications that had gradually eroded his character until he no longer recognized the person staring back at him from mirrors and courthouse windows.

Sleep felt impossible with his mind racing through memories and regrets. Still, exhaustion eventually overcame consciousness, dragging him into dreams filled with courtrooms and airport bars, with faces that belonged to women he'd loved and lost and women he'd desired but couldn't keep. When he woke the next morning, sunlight streaming through blinds that Jennifer had chosen during their first year of marriage, John felt the peculiar emptiness that follows the completion of something that should have been permanent.

He was a divorced man now, officially and legally separated from the woman who'd been his wife, his partner, his closest friend before becoming his greatest disappointment and most profound regret. The apartment that had once represented their shared future now felt like a museum of their failed past, filled with furniture and memories that would need to be reorganized or replaced as he learned to live alone again.

The day stretched ahead with no particular obligations or expectations, the kind of freedom that had once seemed appealing but now felt overwhelming. John had nowhere he needed to be, no one depending on his presence, no shared responsibilities to anchor his time and attention. It was liberation and isolation in equal measure, the double-edged blessing of a life that had been simplified through loss rather than choice.

He made coffee in the machine Jennifer had insisted they needed, checked his phone for messages that didn't come, and began the slow work of figuring out who he was when he wasn't someone's husband, someone's partner, someone's greatest disappointment. The answer, he suspected, would take longer to discover than the marriage had taken to destroy.

Five years later - Present day

The apartment had evolved into something that reflected John's current existence—functional, clean, and deliberately empty of the memories that had once crowded every surface. He sat on his couch, staring at a television screen without seeing the images that flickered across it, when the doorbell's sharp chime cut through his manufactured peace.

Laura stood in his doorway like salvation, wearing a grocery bag, her smile carrying the particular warmth reserved for siblings who'd survived childhood together and emerged as allies. Early forties suited her—she wore them with the confidence of someone who'd learned to find joy in ordinary moments.

"Hi, my love, I thought I'd stop by and make us something to eat."

John's smile felt rusty from disuse, but he managed to summon something approaching genuine pleasure. "Hey, Laura. Come in."

She moved through his space with practiced familiarity, heading directly to the kitchen, where she began unpacking groceries with the efficiency of someone accustomed to feeding a family. John followed, leaning against the counter with arms crossed—a defensive posture he'd perfected during years of deflecting well-meaning concern.

"I hope you're not making yourself feel obligated to come every other week and cook for me, I'm an adult… I can take care of myself."

Laura's teasing smile was identical to the one she'd worn as a child, stealing cookies from their mother's kitchen. "I know. But I want to make sure you're okay."

Their shared laughter felt like muscle memory—automatic and comforting. Laura began chopping vegetables with the steady rhythm of someone who'd learned to find meditation in mundane tasks, while John watched her hands move with enviable purpose.

"So, how have you been holding up?"

The question was casual, but John recognized the careful way she asked it—the tone their family had perfected for approaching subjects too fragile for direct examination.

"Well, let's see, it's been five years… I finally got a cleaning service I can trust. I have you coming every other week to cook for me, and your husband keeps giving out my number to every single woman he gets in contact with."

Laura's laugh was rich and genuine; the sound filling spaces in his apartment that had grown too accustomed to silence.

"He's still doing that… I told him to stop already. Oh my God, that is so embarrassing."

"As you can see, I have an awesome family who loves me very much, and they won't allow me to wallow in self-pity."

The words carried more truth than John had intended to reveal. His family's relentless care had become both anchor and irritation, keeping him tethered to the world while reminding him constantly of his isolation within it.

"We do love you. The kids love their Uncle John. Jax, Mollie, and Charlie are always asking about you. It's been almost a month since your last visit. So, you need to leave your fancy condo and make your way back to Long Island, mister." The accusation in her voice was gentle but unmistakable. John covered both eyes with his hands, the gesture automatic—learned behavior from years of avoiding uncomfortable truths.

"I know… I'm a bad uncle."

"Look at me… You are not a bad uncle. Do you hear me?"

Laura's voice carried the authority she'd developed as a mother, the tone that brooked no argument from children or younger brothers. John dropped his hands, meeting her gaze with reluctance.

"I was a bad husband. Things are not as bad as the first two years after my divorce, but it's been five years, and I still carry regrets."

The admission felt like bloodletting—necessary but painful. Laura moved closer, her hand finding his arm with the practiced ease of someone who'd spent years providing comfort to those who rarely asked for it.

"Yeah… It's normal to feel that way. There's no timeline; everyone heals in their own time."

"I know. But I can't help feeling like I screwed up."

The words hung between them, simple and devastating in their honesty. Laura studied his face with the intensity she'd once reserved for her children's scraped knees and broken toys—problems she could fix with Band-Aids and patience.

"John, everyone makes mistakes. It's what you do after that… that matters. You can't change the past, but you can learn from it."

"I feel like I'm stuck."

The confession escaped before he could stop it, raw and unfiltered. Laura's expression softened, her hand tightening on his arm.

"You're not stuck. You're processing. Remember in 'The Shawshank Redemption,' when Andy says, 'Get busy living, or get busy dying'? You have to choose to move forward, no matter how hard it seems."

John's smile was the first genuine expression he'd worn all day. "I always knew you had a thing for Morgan Freeman's voice."

Their laughter was easier this time, the tension dissipating like steam from a kettle. But the relief was temporary— shadows had ways of reasserting themselves even in well-lit kitchens.

"But seriously, it's hard to forgive myself. I keep thinking about what I did, how I hurt her. And then... finding out she was with Tom. It twisted the knife."

Laura's face grew serious as her sister's intuition read the deeper currents beneath his words. "I get it, John. The betrayal happened on both sides. But beating yourself up won't change what happened. You have to forgive yourself first."

"How do I do that, Laura? How do I forgive myself for hurting the woman I used to love?"

His voice cracked on the question, revealing fractures he'd spent five years trying to hide. Laura's eyes filled with the particular empathy reserved for family members whose pain couldn't be fixed with casseroles and good intentions.

"It starts with understanding why it happened—not justifying it, but understanding it. You were hurting, and you made a bad choice. But you can't let that define you."

John nodded slowly, processing her words like flight data—information to be analyzed and filed away for future reference.

"Yeah. Maybe you're right."

"And you know what else? Fifty percent of the blame is on her. She was thoting around… so you may have lost her, but she lost you too."

The crude assessment was so unlike Laura's usual diplomatic approach that John almost laughed. Instead, tears welled in his eyes— the first he'd allowed himself in months.

"Thanks, Laura. I needed that."

She pulled him into a hug that smelled like vanilla and safety, holding him with the fierce protectiveness she'd shown when they were children navigating their parents' occasional storms. John allowed himself to sink into the embrace, remembering what it felt like to be comforted without conditions or expectations.

"You're going to get through this, John. And I'm here for you every step of the way."

"I know. And I appreciate it more than you know."

When they separated, Laura's smile carried the particular satisfaction of someone who'd successfully performed emergency emotional surgery. She wiped her hands on his dish towel and surveyed his kitchen with renewed purpose.

"Now, how about we make some dinner? I'm thinking something fancy 'cause I'm in your fancy condo… Baked Shrimp Scampi."

John's smile felt more natural now, warmed by the prospect of shared meals and ordinary conversation. "That sounds perfect."

They began cooking together, their movements developing the easy rhythm of siblings who had learned to work around each other in their childhood kitchens. The apartment filled with the sounds of sizzling butter and casual conversation, transforming the space from mausoleum to home, if only temporarily.

As Laura seasoned the shrimp and John prepared the pasta, he found himself thinking about healing—not as a destination but as a daily choice, made one small decision at a time. Tonight, he would eat dinner with his sister, listen to stories about his niece and nephews, and allow himself to be present in the moment without constantly referencing the past.

Tomorrow would bring its own challenges, as well as its own opportunities for grace or regression. But for now, in the warm light of his kitchen, surrounded by the comfortable chaos of shared cooking, John allowed himself to imagine what it might feel like to forgive himself completely—to finally, truly, get busy living.

CHAPTER 3
MIRROR SHARDS

The aroma of garlic and butter hung heavy in John's apartment, mingling with the faint scent of rosemary from the baked shrimp scampi cooling on their plates. Warm light from the overhead fixture cast a golden glow across the dining table, where John and Laura sat in companionable silence. The ceramic plates clinked softly against silverware as they ate, each lost in their thoughts.

Laura lifted her fork, twirling the pasta with practiced ease. Steam rose from the dish, and she paused, studying John's profile as he chewed slowly, deliberately. Lines of exhaustion etched the corners of his eyes, but something else flickered there—a spark she hadn't seen in months.

"So, what's next for you? Any plans?"

John's shoulders lifted in a casual shrug, but his fingers tightened around his fork. The question hung between them, weighted with possibility and uncertainty.

"I'm going to take it one day at a time. I might even go back to therapy. Since it helped me before."

Laura's head bobbed in approval, and warmth spread across her features. "That sounds like a good idea. And maybe start doing things you enjoy again. Like going hiking with the kids."

A sigh escaped John's lips, carrying the weight of missed opportunities and abandoned traditions. His gaze drifted toward the window, where city lights twinkled in the distance.

"Yeah, we have not done that in a while."

"Then let's go this weekend with the kids. Just like old times." Laura's smile brightened the space between them, genuine and infectious.

John's expression softened, gratitude replacing the tension in his jaw. "I'd like that."

Laura reached for her wine glass, the crystal catching the light as she raised it. The gesture carried a ceremony, a promise.

"To new beginnings."

John mirrored her movement, his glass meeting hers with a delicate chime. The sound reverberated through the apartment, sealing their unspoken pact.

"To new beginnings."

Their smiles reflected each other across the table, hope blooming in the space where despair had once festered. The room itself seemed to exhale, releasing months of accumulated sorrow.

Across Town.

City lights pressed against the windows of Samaya's twenty-sixth-floor apartment in Waterline Square like a living thing. The space bore the hallmarks of careful curation—sleek furniture arranged with precision, abstract art positioned for maximum impact, and ambient lighting that suggested sophistication. Yet beneath the polished surface, emptiness echoed in every corner.

Samaya curled into the corner of her leather couch, her thirty-something frame swallowed by oversized cushions. The blue glow from her phone illuminated her face as she scrolled through digital memories, each swipe revealing another fragment of her romantic history. Photos cascaded past— dinner dates, vacation snapshots, intimate moments captured in pixels and stored like evidence of dreams deferred.

"Here we go again."

The words escaped as a whisper, carrying the weight of patterns she couldn't seem to break. She set the phone aside and unfolded herself from the couch, bare feet silent against the hardwood floor. The kitchen beckoned with its promise of liquid solace.

Wine splashed into the glass with a sound like rain against pavement. The first sip burned slightly, warming her throat and spreading heat through her chest. She leaned against the granite counter, letting the alcohol blur the sharp edges of memory.

Two years earlier...

The restaurant had been dimly lit, intimate in the way expensive places manufactured romance. Jake sat across from her, his handsome features twisted with an anger that made her stomach clench. His voice carried the authority of someone accustomed to compliance.

"I told you; I don't want you hanging out with those friends of yours. They're a bad influence."

Samaya's spine straightened, defiance flaring despite her racing heart. "They're my friends, Jake. You can't dictate who I can and can't see."

"I'm just looking out for you. You should be grateful." His tone dripped with condescension; each word was designed to diminish her.

"This isn't love, Jake. This is control." The truth tasted bitter on her tongue, but she couldn't swallow it anymore.

Jake's expression hardened, his eyes becoming chips of ice.

"Maybe you don't know what love is."

Later that same night...

Tears had streamed down Samaya's face as she pressed the phone to her ear, her voice breaking with each sob. The apartment around her felt suffocating, walls closing in with the weight of Jake's words.

"I don't know what to do, Valou. He makes me feel so small, like I'm worthless."

Valouna's voice carried across the line like a lifeline, warm and steady. "You need to leave him, Samee. You deserve so much better."

"I know, but it's so hard. I feel like I'm stuck." The admission had torn from her throat, raw and desperate.

Six months later...

The coffee shop buzzed with the energy of the afternoon, but Mark's attention remained fixed on his phone screen. His fingers moved across the device with practiced efficiency; each tap was another small betrayal. Samaya watched him from across the table, her heart sinking with familiar disappointment.

"Mark, are you even listening to me?"

His eyes flicked up briefly, irritation creasing his brow. "Yeah, yeah, I'm listening."

"I just feel like you're not present anymore. Like you're always somewhere else." The words carried the exhaustion of someone tired of fighting for scraps of attention.

Mark's dismissive wave cut through her concerns like a blade. "You're imagining things, Baby. Everything's fine." The night she discovered the truth...

The text messages had glowed on Mark's phone screen like neon signs of betrayal. Each word drove deeper into her chest, confirming suspicions she'd tried to ignore. When she confronted him, he didn't even have the decency to lie.

"Yeah, I've been seeing someone else. So what?"

The casual cruelty in his voice had stolen her breath. "How could you do this to me?"

His cold smile cut through her heart. "Because you let me." And after Mark, there was David...

The bar had thrummed with music and conversation, creating a cocoon of artificial intimacy. David's charm worked like a drug, making her forget the warnings her friends had whispered. His smile could have melted steel.

"You know, you're really special, luv."

Heat had risen in her cheeks at the compliment, hope blooming despite her better judgment. "Thanks, David. That means a lot."

David sipped his whiskey, ice clinking against the glass. "But I'm not ready for anything serious right now."

The words hit like cold water, washing away her burgeoning feelings.

"I thought we had something good going."

"We do. I just don't want to be tied down." His casual shrug dismissed months of building a connection.

"I'm not asking you to be tied down. I just want to know where we stand."

Frustration leaked into her voice despite her efforts to remain calm.

David leaned back in his chair, creating physical distance to match his emotional retreat. "We stand where we stand. Let's not complicate things."

And before all of them, there had been Peter...

Her bedroom felt like a shrine to lost love as she held the photograph, its edges worn soft from handling. Peter's kind eyes stared back at her from the frame, capturing a moment when happiness had seemed possible.

He was different, she thought. Kind, caring, but we weren't meant to be.

Their final walk...

The air had been soft that evening, not quite warm, not quite cold—just enough to make the moment feel like it was holding its breath.

Their hands were still intertwined, but something had changed. Not distance… not yet. Just a quiet hesitation, like neither of them wanted to be the first to let go.

Samaya could feel the weight of his hand in hers—familiar, steady—but it didn't feel the same anymore. It felt like something slipping, something neither of them knew how to hold onto.

For a while, neither of them spoke.

And somehow, that silence said more than anything they were about to admit. They walked hand-in-hand down the winding path, but the space between them yawned wider with each step. Peter's voice carried the weight of a difficult truth.

"I love you, Baby. But I feel like we're going in different directions."

She had nodded, recognizing the inevitable in his words. "I feel it too. I guess we've grown apart."

"I'll always care about you." His sincerity made the goodbye both easier and harder to bear.

"And I'll always care about you, too." The smile she'd given him had been genuine, tinged with sadness but free of regret.

Present day...

Samaya returned to the couch, wine glass in hand, and caught her reflection in the dark window. The woman staring back looked tired, worn down by the weight of repeated disappointments. Her gaze shifted to a photograph on the side table—her and Valouna outside a nightclub, both radiant with youth and possibility.

"You deserve better. You deserve her, but she's too chicken shit to allow herself to be happy."

The words emerged as a whisper, a confession to the empty room. She picked up her phone and scrolled to a familiar number, her thumb hovering over the call button before pressing it.

The phone rang once, twice, three times before Valouna's voice filled the silence.

"Hey, Samee. What's up?"

"Hey, Valou, my love. Just wanted to hear a friendly voice." Samaya's voice carried exhaustion like a physical weight.

"I'm always here for you. How are you holding up?" Warmth radiated through the phone, enveloping Samaya like an embrace.

She sighed, settling deeper into the cushions. "Just reflecting on things. I've made some bad choices, and I'm tired. I say you marry me now so I can avoid making another one."

Valouna's laugh carried affection and exasperation in equal measure. "Samee, my love, I told you I can't afford you. But if ever I get rich, I would so marry you."

Tears gathered in Samaya's eyes, hope and frustration warring in her chest. "Why don't you leave Queens and come to the city tonight and let me love on you. It's been too long."

"Samee, I can't. It took me damn near these last 2 years to remove our last encounter from my head. If I go there again with you, it would be hard for me to get back to reality." Valouna's voice carried the weight of self-preservation, of boundaries drawn in permanent ink.

"And why would you want to go back to reality if you had me to love you?" The question hung in the air, desperate and raw.

The phone's second line began ringing, its insistent tone cutting through their conversation. Samaya glanced at the caller ID, her heart lurching at the familiar name.

"Oh my God, Peter is calling me, I'll call you back, girl."

She ended the call with Valouna and switched lines, her finger trembling slightly as she accepted Peter's call.

On the other end of the disconnected line, Valouna held the phone to her ear for a long moment, listening to the silence where Samaya's voice had been.

"This is why I won't participate in your experiment. You're too boy crazy. I need guarantees you're not prepared to give me."

The words fell into empty air, unheard but necessary, a boundary maintained through distance and discipline.

Morning light streamed through the cockpit windows of the commercial airliner, illuminating the array of instruments and controls that John had navigated countless times before. His hands moved with practiced precision through the preflight checks, muscle memory guiding each switch and dial. Beside him, Captain Adam matched his methodical pace.

"All systems look good, Captain. Ready for another smooth flight?"

John's grin cut through the professional atmosphere, revealing the passion that had drawn him to aviation decades earlier. "Always ready. Let's get this bird in the air."

Behind them, the main cabin filled with the controlled chaos of boarding passengers. Carry-on luggage thudded into overhead compartments while flight attendants moved through the aisles with practiced efficiency. Among the steady stream of travelers, Samaya made her way down the narrow aisle, her movements deliberate despite the exhaustion etched in the lines around her eyes.

She located her assigned seat and settled into the worn fabric, pulling a paperback novel from her purse. The book's pages showed evidence of multiple readings, its spine cracked from repeated openings. She opened to a dog-eared page and tried to lose herself in someone else's story, seeking refuge from the weight of her own.

In the cockpit, John completed his final checks and leaned back in his captain's chair. The aircraft hummed around him, a living thing preparing for flight. Brief silence settled over the flight deck before the intercom crackled to life.

"Captain, the passengers are all aboard. Ready for takeoff when you are."

John's finger found the radio switch, his voice carrying the calm authority of thousands of successful flights. "Copy that. Let's get moving."

The engines spooled up with a deep rumble that vibrated through the aircraft's frame, power building for the moment when metal would defy gravity once again. In the cabin, Samaya closed her book and gazed out the small window as the ground began to move past, carrying her toward whatever waited beyond the horizon.

CHAPTER 4
SKYBOUND TENSIONS

The aircraft shuddered slightly as it began its taxi toward the runway, metal groaning against tarmac. Samaya pressed her palm against the small window, watching ground crews scatter like ants as the massive jet rolled forward. Her pulse quickened with the familiar thrill of takeoff—that moment when tons of steel would defy gravity through sheer force and engineering precision.

The engines roared to life, their deep rumble vibrating through her seat and into her bones. She gripped the armrest as the plane accelerated down the runway, buildings and cars shrinking to miniature proportions outside her window. The aircraft lifted with surprising grace, leaving the earth behind in a rush of power and momentum.

As Miami fell away beneath them, Samaya glanced at her watch—barely an hour into the flight. She opened her paperback novel, its familiar weight comforting in her hands, and tried to lose herself in someone else's story. The words blurred slightly as her mind wandered to the phone call with Peter the night before, to Valouna's distant voice, to the endless cycle of disappointment that seemed to define her romantic life.

In the cockpit, John's hands moved across the instrument panel with practiced efficiency, checking altitude, airspeed, and navigation systems. The aircraft had reached its cruising altitude of thirty-seven thousand feet, stable and steady in the thin air above the clouds. He flipped the autopilot switch, the soft click confirming the computer's control over their trajectory.

"I'll do the rounds. Keep an eye on things here."

Captain Adam nodded without lifting his gaze from the flight displays. "Roger that."

John unbuckled his harness and stood, stretching muscles cramped from the confined cockpit space. The main cabin awaited—rows of passengers settling into the rhythm of flight, some sleeping, others reading, a few staring out windows at the endless expanse of sky.

He moved down the narrow aisle with the measured pace of someone comfortable in his authority. Passengers glanced up as he passed, some nodding politely, others returning to their private worlds. Near the middle of the cabin, his attention snagged on a familiar silhouette—a woman absorbed in her book, dark hair catching the overhead light. Those legs look amazingly familiar. He prides himself on being a leg connoisseur.

Something stirred in his chest, a recognition he couldn't quite place.

"Enjoying the flight?"

Samaya's head snapped up, surprise flickering across her features as she registered the captain's uniform, the friendly smile, the unexpected attention.

"Oh… yes. It's been great so far. Thanks."

John's smile deepened, genuine warmth replacing professional courtesy. "Glad to hear it. Anything I can get you to make your flight more pleasant?"

"I'm a simple girl. Just get us to Miami in one piece and I'll be happy." Her voice carried a softness that matched her understated beauty—no excessive makeup, no designer clothes demanding attention, simply a woman comfortable in her own skin.

"Don't worry, you're in good hands." The words carried conviction earned through thousands of successful flights and countless passengers delivered safely to their destinations.

He moved on, but something made him glance over his shoulder. Samaya watched him retreat down the aisle, curiosity evident in her expression. Their brief exchange had sparked an unexpected and intriguing connection.

The galley hummed with quiet activity as flight attendant Kate prepared beverage service. Steam rose from the coffee pot, rich aroma mingling with the recycled air. She handed John a ceramic mug, the liquid dark and strong.

"So, Captain, any plans after we land?"

John accepted the coffee gratefully, the warmth seeping through the cup into his palms. "Just the usual. Maybe catch a movie, unwind a bit."

Kate's smirk carried years of friendly banter between colleagues. "Still on that romantic comedy kick?"

"What can I say? I'm a sucker for a good love story." His grin acknowledged the gentle teasing while revealing something deeper—a man who believed in romance despite evidence to the contrary.

Footsteps approached from the main cabin. Samaya appeared in the galley entrance, her movement fluid despite the aircraft's subtle vibrations. John noticed her at first glance; the conversation with Kate needed to end immediately.

"You should try something new. Maybe an adventure film. You know, spice things up."

John chuckled, but his attention remained divided. "I'll consider it." He held one finger in the air.

"Hold that thought." He turned toward Samaya, who offered a polite smile that didn't quite mask her underlying nervousness.

"Sorry to interrupt. Just needed some water."

"No interruption at all. Here, let me get you that." John reached for a bottle of water, their fingers brushing briefly as he handed it to her. The contact sent an unexpected jolt through his system.

"Thanks. By the way, what's your favorite romantic comedy?"

The question surprised him with its directness, its implicit suggestion of shared interests. "Probably 'When Harry Met Sally.' Classic, right?"

Samaya's laugh transformed her face, erasing the careful composure and revealing genuine delight. "A man with taste.

That's one of my favorites, too."

For a second, neither of them said anything. It wasn't awkward. It just… lingered. Like they had both stepped into something they didn't fully understand yet. John noticed the way her expression softened when she smiled less guarded, more present. It wasn't the kind of reaction he was used to getting. There was no performance in it.

And Samaya felt it too. Not attraction. Not yet. Just a quiet awareness… that this moment mattered more than it should have.

The moment stretched between them, filled with possibility. John found himself stepping closer to the edge of professional boundaries, drawn by an attraction he couldn't explain.

"Then I guess I'll have to rewatch it… Maybe I can get your number to call you to let you know which part I still find captivating."

Samaya's gaze traveled the length of his frame—broad shoulders filling the captain's uniform, steady hands that had guided aircraft through storms, eyes that promised reliability and adventure in equal measure. Her teeth caught her bottom lip, a gesture unconsciously sensual.

"Are you sure you want my number?"

"Absolutely."

The single word carried weight, certainty, and intent. Something shifted in the narrow galley space, professional distance collapsing into personal territory.

Hours later, the cabin had settled into the quiet rhythm of night flight. Most passengers slept beneath thin airline blankets, while others gazed out the windows at the star-scattered darkness. Samaya remained awake; her book forgotten in her lap as thoughts churned through her mind.

The brief encounter with John had unsettled her carefully constructed equilibrium. After years of disappointing relationships, she'd grown wary of attraction, suspicious of chemistry that promised more than it delivered. Yet something about the captain felt different—grounded where others had been flighty, steady where others had proven unreliable.

She glanced toward the cockpit, where John worked behind the closed door. The aircraft now flew itself, but pilots remained vigilant, monitoring systems and weather, ready to intervene if the automation failed. The responsibility was enormous—hundreds of lives depending on his skill and judgment.

In the cockpit, John maintained his professional facade while his thoughts drifted to the woman in seat 12C. Adam caught the slight smile playing at the corners of his mouth, years of flying together making him sensitive to his captain's moods.

"What's with the smile, Captain?"

John's expression remained carefully neutral. "Just thinking about this movie I'm catching up on."

Adam's grin suggested he wasn't fooled. "Sure, you are."

The gentle teasing bounced off John harmlessly. His mind had already moved beyond the current flight, imagining possibilities that began with a phone number exchanged at thirty-seven thousand feet.

Three days later...

Samaya's apartment enveloped her like a familiar friend, the warm light casting golden circles across the hardwood floors. She'd changed from her work clothes into comfortable jeans and a soft sweater that brought out the brown in her eyes. The phone buzzed against the coffee table, John's name illuminating the screen.

Excitement fluttered in her chest as she answered. "Hi, John!"

"Hey, Samaya! How's it going?" His voice carried the same warmth she remembered from their brief encounter, now filtered through the static of a telephone and digital compression.

"I was just thinking about you. What a nice surprise!" The admission slipped out before she could censor it, honesty trumping careful game-playing.

"I'm glad I could brighten your evening. I've been thinking about you now that you're back in New York. I was hoping we could go somewhere and talk."

Curiosity sharpened her attention. "Oh? What's on your mind?"

There are so many great restaurants in the city. Maybe you and I can finally go on a date together." His enthusiasm carried across the phone line, infectious and endearing.

Surprise and excitement warred in her chest. "Oh my gosh, John! That sounds amazing! I'd love to go out with you."

Relief colored his response. "Fantastic! I've been thinking of a place that's both charming and relaxing. There's this quaint little bistro downtown—Cozy Corner Café. It has a great atmosphere, perfect for a romantic evening. They have these incredible candlelit tables and a menu that's supposed to be out of this world. What do you think?"

"That sounds perfect! I've heard great things about Cozy Corner Café. I can't wait." Her voice carried the breathless quality of someone allowing hope to take root despite past disappointments.

"Awesome. How about this Saturday evening? We can have a leisurely dinner and then maybe take a stroll around the city afterward. I know a lovely park nearby where we can walk and talk."

"Saturday evening sounds wonderful. I'm already looking forward to it. It's been ages since I've had a night like that." The longing in her voice revealed more than she intended about the drought of meaningful connection in her life.

"I promise to make it a night to remember."

"Just be yourself, John. I'm really looking forward to getting to know you better." The simple request carried profound weight—an invitation to authenticity in a world of careful personas and strategic self-presentation.

"I am, too. I just have a feeling this is the start of something really special. So, let's make it a night full of laughter and great conversations."

"I wouldn't want it any other way. Thank you for asking me out. It means a lot." Gratitude threaded through her words, acknowledgment of the courage required to reach across the space between strangers.

"I'm glad. It's going to be a great evening. I'll pick you up around 7?"

"Sounds perfect. I'll be ready." She could already imagine herself getting ready, choosing the right dress, the right perfume, the right version of herself to present.

"Like I told you before, it's been five years since I've been on a date. So, I need assurance that I get a do-over card if it wasn't magical for you."

The vulnerability in his admission touched something deep in her chest. Here was a successful man, confident in his professional life, revealing uncertainty about romance. The honesty was refreshing after years of men who pretended to be infallible.

"I'm sure I'm going to have a smile on my face from beginning to end."

"You think too highly of me. I want to cancel our date."

The playful threat made her laugh. "If you cancel our date, you might as well delete my number from your phone. 'Cause

I can't wait to see you again."

"Then I guess our date is back on."

The call ended, leaving Samaya glowing with anticipation. She settled deeper into her couch, replaying their conversation, already imagining Saturday evening. Hope unfurled in her chest like a flower reaching toward sunlight— fragile, precious, and surprisingly resilient.

Saturday evening...

The Cozy Corner Café lived up to its name, with intimate tables scattered throughout the brick-walled space like islands of privacy. Candles flickered in glass holders, casting dancing shadows across white tablecloths. The gentle murmur of conversation provided a backdrop to the soft jazz playing through hidden speakers.

John and Samaya sat across from each other at a corner table, partially eaten gourmet dishes pushed aside to make room for wine glasses and intertwined fingers. The initial nervousness had long since evaporated, replaced by the comfortable rhythm of two people discovering unexpected compatibility.

"You know, I almost didn't show up tonight. Just 'cause you made that joke the other day. I wanted to teach you a lesson."

John's eyebrow lifted, smile wavering between amusement and concern. "I'm sorry, when I find somebody, I really like, I tend to say stupid jokes."

"Hey, I'm joking… don't get so serious." She leaned across the table and pressed her lips to his, the kiss soft but deliberate. The contact sent electricity through both of them, the restaurant around them temporarily forgotten.

"You don't need a do-over card. I think you're doing great." His grin returned, confidence restored. "You don't have to tell me what I already know… was there any doubt?"

She lifted her wine glass, eyes meeting his over the rim as she sipped. The burgundy liquid stained her lips slightly, adding color to her already flushed cheeks. "No doubts at all."

Their laughter mingled with the ambient sounds of the restaurant, creating a bubble of intimacy within the public space. The waiter refilled their water glasses unnoticed as they lost themselves in each other's gaze.

Samaya leaned back, crossing her legs with deliberate grace. The movement was unconsciously sensual, drawing John's attention to the elegant line of her calves, the way the candlelight played across her skin.

"To me, legs are the sexiest part of a woman's body. That's what attracts me to a woman first. And you have the most beautiful legs I've ever seen in my life. But I want your legs to be the 13th thing I find most attractive in you."

The unexpected compliment caught her off guard, curiosity replacing surprise. "Wait, if my legs are the sexiest you have ever seen in the entire world… what would be the 12 features you would put before them?"

John's expression grew serious, the playful banter shifting into something deeper. "It's true your legs should be in the Guinness Book of Records. But I want to love your passion, your devotion, your emotion, your intelligence, your elegance, your courage, your kindness, your humbleness, your honesty, and your love more than I love what most people would place in their top 3… which is your face, your smile, and your legs. I want to love you so deeply that those things couldn't even crack the top 20 most extraordinary things I would love about you."

Silence stretched between them, charged with possibility and promise. Samaya's fingers played with the stem of her wine glass; the gesture was unconsciously sensual as she processed his words. No man had ever spoken to her with such depth, such genuine desire for connection beyond the physical.

"I… so want to fuck you right now."

The words escaped before she could stop them, raw desire overriding careful restraint. John's eyes widened, surprise and arousal warring in his expression. The air between them crackled with sexual tension, the restaurant's ambient noise fading into background static.

Their connection had crossed into dangerous territory, professional boundaries and social niceties forgotten in the face of pure attraction. Without speaking, they both understood where the evening was heading, the inevitable pull of chemistry too strong to resist.

ACT II
The Unraveling

CHAPTER 5
HIDDEN DEPTHS

The apartment door crashed open with desperate momentum. John's keys clattered against the hardwood floor as he and Samee stumbled across the threshold, a tangle of limbs and urgent desire. The dim hallway light caught the flush across Samee's cheekbones; her lipstick smeared from their heated exchange in the restaurant's parking lot. Her designer heels clicked an erratic rhythm against the wood before one caught the edge of his area rug.

She pitched forward with a breathless laugh, but John's arms snaked around her waist, steadying her against his chest. The scent of her perfume—jasmine and something darker— mixed with the lingering aroma of wine on their breath. Their eyes locked in the amber glow from the street lamp filtering through his seventeen floor windows. No words passed between them. None were needed.

His mouth found hers again, hungry and insistent. Her fingers fisted in his shirt, tugging him deeper into the apartment as they moved like dancers caught in some primal choreography. The coffee table scraped against the hardwood as they navigated around it, their bodies pressed together, hands exploring with increasing urgency.

Her blazer slipped from her shoulders and puddled on the floor beside his discarded tie. The city hummed its nighttime symphony beyond the windows—distant sirens, the occasional car horn, the murmur of late-night conversations drifting up from the street—but inside John's apartment, only their ragged breathing filled the silence between fevered kisses.

"We should... slow down... right?" Samee's words emerged in fragments between kisses, her voice breathy and uncertain even as her body pressed closer to his.

John pulled back slightly, his chest rising and falling as he searched her face. A slow grin spread across his features, his eyes dark with want. "You want to?"

Rather than answer with words, Samee's hands found the back of his neck, her fingers threading through his hair as she drew him down to her. Her mouth claimed his with renewed intensity, erasing any doubt about her intentions.

After midnight…

Streetlight painted silver stripes across the bedroom walls through the partially closed blinds, casting everything in alternating bars of pale light and shadow. The sheets lay twisted and forgotten, draped half off the mattress where they had been kicked aside in passion's wake—expensive Egyptian cotton that John had bought specifically for tonight, now wrinkled and abandoned like discarded clothing. John's chest rose and fell in a steady rhythm as sleep tried to claim him, but Samee's weight against his shoulder kept him anchored in the present moment.

Her fingers traced lazy patterns across his skin, following the contours of muscle and bone with absent-minded precision. Each touch sent small electric currents through his nervous system, reminders of what they had just shared. The apartment had settled into post-midnight quiet, broken only by the slight distant hum of car horns and ambulance sirens seventeen floors below and the occasional creak of old pipes in the walls. John could smell her perfume mixed with sweat and something else—something that belonged to both of them now.

He had been replaying every moment in his mind: the way she had looked at him across the dinner table earlier, the electric tension during the cab ride home, her hand on his knee as they took the elevator to his apartment. Everything had felt choreographed by some benevolent universe, each moment flowing seamlessly into the next. He was already composing the story he would tell his friends, already imagining future evenings that would begin just like this one.

Samee's fingers slowed against his skin.

For a moment, she stayed still, her cheek resting lightly against his shoulder, her gaze fixed somewhere beyond the ceiling.

Something wasn't sitting right.

It should have felt different.

It should have stayed with her.

But instead… there was a quiet emptiness she couldn't ignore.

And she hated that feeling.

Because she knew exactly what it meant.

"That wasn't boring." The words emerged from her throat like a casual observation about the weather. "But it wasn't fulfilling."

The statement dropped into the silence like stones into still water, creating ripples of confusion across John's consciousness. He felt the words register first as sound, then as meaning, then as something that fundamentally altered the molecular structure of the air between them.

He had been floating in the afterglow of what he considered the most transcendent experience of his adult life. Every nerve ending still hummed with the memory of her touch, every breath still carried traces of her presence. Her declaration hit him like cold water, jolting him fully awake and stripping away the golden haze that had enveloped the last two hours. The magic he thought they had shared seemed to evaporate in the space between her words and his comprehension, leaving behind something clinical and detached.

John's laugh came out strained, a sound that belonged in a different conversation entirely—one where he wasn't suddenly scrambling to understand what had gone wrong. Embarrassment crept up his neck like heat rash, spreading across his chest and face with uncomfortable warmth. He fought to maintain his equilibrium, to project the confidence he didn't actually possess, the ease he had felt just moments before.

"I'll do better next time," he managed, the words sounding hollow even to his own ears. The promise hung in the air, desperate and slightly pathetic.

"I know you will." Samee's voice carried a matter-of-fact certainty, as if she were confirming an appointment or agreeing to meet for coffee. There was no malice in her tone, no cruelty—just a practical acknowledgment of future improvement that somehow made everything worse.

She untangled herself from the sheets with fluid efficiency, her movements suddenly purposeful rather than languid. John watched the curve of her spine as she stood, memorizing the way the streetlight caught the slope of her shoulders. She padded toward the bathroom without looking back, her footsteps soft against the hardwood floor he had spent an entire Saturday refinishing.

The shower turned on moments later, and through the thin walls— walls he had never noticed were thin until this moment—he heard the unmistakable sound of her voice. Not singing, not humming, but speaking in low, measured tones. The words were indistinct, but the cadence was familiar: brief, clipped instructions to an Uber driver. She was already planning her exit while steam fogged the mirror he looked into every morning.

John stared at the ceiling, cataloging every crack in the plaster, listening to the water run, and trying to process what had shifted in the span of minutes. The same ceiling that had witnessed what he thought was the beginning of something significant now seemed to mock his naivety. The evening had felt like a beginning—the kind of night that changes trajectories, that becomes part of a larger story about how two people found each other. Now it felt like something else entirely: a brief intersection, a momentary pause in her larger journey, already forgotten while the water was still running.

He wondered if she would remember his name in a week. He wondered if he had already become part of a pattern he couldn't see, a story she would tell differently—or perhaps not tell at all. The apartment felt larger now, emptier, as if her departure had already begun even while she was still there, washing away the evidence of their evening with hotel-grade efficiency.

Through the bathroom door, he heard her phone buzz again—probably the driver, already waiting downstairs. John closed his eyes and tried to hold onto something from the night that felt real, something that belonged to him alone. But even his memories felt different now, viewed through the lens of her casual dismissal, transformed from transcendent to merely adequate with five simple words.

The water stopped running.

Samaya's living room basked in morning sunlight that streamed through floor-to-ceiling windows, illuminating dust motes dancing in the air. The space reflected its owner's personality in curated details—shelves lined with dog-eared paperbacks, framed photographs clustered on the mantle, and succulents thriving in geometric planters scattered throughout the room.

Samee sat cross-legged on the cream-colored sectional, her energy radiating outward in animated gestures and bright expressions. Steam rose from two ceramic mugs on the glass coffee table between her and Valouna, who had claimed the opposite corner of the couch with characteristic reserve.

Where Samee buzzed with caffeinated enthusiasm, Valouna embodied stillness. She leaned into the cushions with feline grace, her dark eyes studying her friend's face as she listened to the recap of the previous evening's events.

"We went on our first date last night and I ended up in his apartment." Samee's declaration hung in the air between them like a confession seeking absolution.

Valouna's eyebrows rose in perfect arcs above her coffee mug. She took a deliberate sip, using the pause to choose her response with characteristic precision.

"You did it on the first date... really, Samee... is that what I taught you to do?"

Samee's hands flew to cover her face, but her smile leaked through her fingers. "I blame the fact that you don't give me any anymore. I have needs, woman, don't judge me... in fact, you have to meet him. He's a charmer, this one."

The words carried layers of meaning, references to their shared history painted in casual tones. Valouna shifted uncomfortably, her posture stiffening as she placed her mug on the table with unnecessary care.

"I don't want to feel like a third wheel, Samee. You and John are still in that... early stage. Let your relationship grow stronger before you introduce me."

"Don't flatter yourself, he's not into hairy armpit women. I want you to get to know him and nothing more." Samee's playful nudge accompanied the teasing words, but beneath the surface, currents of something deeper moved between them.

Valouna exhaled slowly, her internal conflict playing out in the tension across her shoulders. She uncrossed her arms, then crossed them again, her gaze shifting between Samee's expectant face and the coffee growing cold in her mug.

"Please let him know I'm coming on your date. I hate when they stare at me like I'm here to cockblock them."

"Absolutely. I will definitely tell him. But Valou, my love, please shave your armpits. The feminist shit you on... only I love this shit. I don't want to pay for anything but my dress tonight."

Valouna's sigh held the weight of surrender. She glanced down at her reflection in the coffee's dark surface before meeting Samee's eyes with reluctant agreement.

"Fine. I'll shave my armpits. I'll even take a shower with soap."

"Yes! My lover is back... I miss you!" Samee's hands clapped together in childlike delight as she launched herself across the couch to envelope Valouna in an enthusiastic embrace.

Valouna rolled her eyes with practiced affection, but curiosity flickered across her features as she allowed herself to be pulled into the hug. The embrace lingered longer than casual friendship typically warranted, speaking to intimacies and history neither woman named aloud.

"I'll text you the details. Wear something cute, okay?" Samee bounced off the couch with renewed energy, already mentally planning the evening's orchestration.

Valouna shook her head with amused resignation, watching her friend's excitement with the indulgent expression of someone accustomed to being swept along in Samee's wake.

The trendy bar pulsed with urban energy—conversations layered over the steady thrum of bass-heavy music, while Edison bulbs cast warm circles of light across exposed brick walls. John and Samee occupied a high-top table near the center of the action, their second date unfolding with the easy rhythm of growing attraction.

John's beer sat half-empty beside Samee's wine glass, their conversation flowing between comfortable silences and shared laughter. The evening carried promise, a natural progression from their first encounter, until Samee's attention shifted toward the entrance.

Her face lit up with recognition as she spotted someone threading their way through the crowd. John followed her gaze, confusion creasing his features as he watched Valouna scan the room with obvious purpose.

"Valouna! Over here!" Samee's enthusiastic wave cut through the ambient noise.

Valouna approached their table with measured steps, her smile polite but reserved. John rose reflexively, his beer sloshing slightly as he tried to process this unexpected development.

"Oh, hey! You must be Valouna." His greeting carried forced cheer over genuine bewilderment.

"Yeah, that's me. Nice to finally meet you, John." Valouna's response held professional warmth as she settled into the chair Samee had somehow managed to procure from a neighboring table.

John reclaimed his seat; his smile strained around the edges. "Nice to meet you, too. Samee's told me a lot about you."

"Hopefully, all good things." Valouna's eyebrow arched with playful challenge.

"Of course! Only good things. I thought it'd be fun for us all to hang out tonight. Valou, been wanting to meet you anyway." Samee's explanation carried the breezy confidence of someone orchestrating events according to her own mysterious logic.

John nodded along, but uncertainty flickered in his eyes like candlelight in a draft. This wasn't the intimate second date he had envisioned. The dynamics had shifted, leaving him feeling like an observer in his own romantic life. He took a longer pull from his beer, studying the interplay between the two women as they slipped into familiar conversational rhythms.

"You didn't mention I'd be crashing date night." Valouna's words carried a gentle accusation wrapped in humor.

"Please, you're not crashing. You're enhancing." Samee's response came with characteristic deflection.

Their laughter created its own bubble of intimacy, one where John existed on the periphery. He watched their easy rapport with growing fascination and mild irritation, trying to decode the undercurrents flowing between them.

Samee seemed to register his exclusion, turning back to him with renewed attention. "John, Valou loves art. You should tell her about the gallery you visited last week. The one with the abstract stuff? I bet she'd be into it."

The lifeline offered him a way back into the conversation. John straightened, eager to contribute something meaningful to the evening. "Oh, yeah, it was a cool spot. They had some really unique pieces. You're into abstract art?"

"Definitely. I've always loved how abstract art leaves so much room for interpretation. It's like everyone can see something different in the same piece." Valouna's response carried genuine enthusiasm, the first unguarded emotion she had displayed since arriving.

"Exactly! This is what I love about it, too. There was a painting with all these crazy, swirling dark colors, and it reminded me of the sky at dusk. But someone else saw it as, like, an ocean wave crashing." John found his rhythm, his passion for the subject overriding his earlier discomfort.

Valouna's eyes brightened with authentic interest, and the conversation began to flow naturally between them. Samee settled back in her chair with visible satisfaction, watching her two favorite people discover common ground.

"See? I knew you two would hit it off." Her grin held proprietary pride.

As the evening progressed, John found himself drawn into increasingly animated discussions with Valouna about art, films, and shared cultural touchstones. The strangeness of the situation didn't entirely fade—this remained the most unconventional second date of his experience—but he couldn't deny his growing intrigue with Samee's enigmatic friend.

Valouna's initial reserve melted away as they discovered mutual interests and complementary perspectives. Her wit proved sharp, yet never cutting; her observations were insightful without being pretentious. She and John built conversational bridges while Samee served as both audience and occasional contributor, clearly pleased with the evening's trajectory.

Cool night air hit their faces as they emerged from the bar's warmth onto the sidewalk. The city stretched around them in all directions, alive with neon signs and the distant rumble of late-night traffic. Samee immediately claimed John's arm, threading hers through his with casual possession as they began walking down the tree-lined street.

Valouna fell into step beside them, her earlier hesitation replaced by something approaching contentment. The three of them moved together like old friends, their conversation continuing to flow over the urban soundtrack of their surroundings.

"See? Not so bad, right? You two practically have your own secret club now." Samee's teasing carried genuine warmth as she looked between her companions.

"Yeah, you're right. John's not as boring as I thought he'd be." Valouna's smirk softened the mock insult.

John's laughter echoed off the buildings around them. "I'll take that as a compliment."

Samee leaned her head against John's shoulder as they walked, her contentment evident in the relaxed line of her body. "I told you guys this would be fun. We should do this again sometime."

Valouna offered a noncommittal shrug, but her glance toward John carried unmistakable interest. The evening had transformed from awkward intrusion into something more complex—a triangle of attraction and friendship with boundaries yet to be defined.

The city lights blurred around them as they walked deeper into the night, three people bound together by circumstances none of them had anticipated. Behind them, the bar's neon sign flickered against the darkness, marking the place where their unlikely dynamic had taken its first tentative steps toward something entirely unexpected.

CHAPTER 6
CROSSING LINES

The restaurant's amber light flickered across their faces like whispered secrets. Candle wax dripped steadily onto the worn wooden table between the three of them, creating small pools of hardened memories from previous evenings shared by other couples, other triangles of attraction and uncertainty. The booth's cracked leather embraced them in forced intimacy while outside, the city's pulse continued its relentless rhythm.

Samee's wine glass caught the candlelight as she lifted it to her lips, her attention drifting between her phone's glowing screen and the animated conversation unfolding across from her. The familiar weight of exclusion settled around her shoulders like an unwelcome shawl. Her companions had discovered a frequency she couldn't quite tune into, their words bouncing between them with electric precision.

"No way! You actually think 'The Godfather Part II' is better than the first one?" Valouna's grin transformed her usually reserved features into something radiant and unguarded.

John's laughter rumbled through the restaurant's ambient noise—the clink of silverware against ceramic, distant conversations, the gentle jazz bleeding from hidden speakers. He shrugged with the casual confidence of someone defending a beloved position. "I mean, yeah! The whole storyline with Vito's rise is amazing. Plus, Al Pacino's performance in Part II is... unmatched."

Wine slid down Samee's throat, bitter and necessary. She glanced between them with eyes that smiled while her chest tightened with an emotion she refused to name. "I never got the hype about those movies. Too long. Too dark."

Her comment landed like a pebble thrown into rushing water—acknowledged but ultimately swept away by the current of their enthusiasm. John's chuckle carried no malice, but his focus remained magnetized toward Valouna's animated features.

"But seriously, don't you think the storytelling was way more complex in the second one?" John leaned forward, his elbows bracketing his untouched pasta.

"Exactly! It's not a sequel for the sake of a sequel. It dives deeper into the characters, especially Michael's transformation. It's iconic." Valouna's hands moved as she spoke, painting invisible pictures in the air between them.

Samee fidgeted with her napkin, twisting the linen between her fingers as she observed their effortless rapport. The connection sparked between them like exposed electrical wires, dangerous and undeniable. For a moment, she drifted into the space between waking and dreaming, where possibilities bloomed like flowers in accelerated time.

"Okay, you two, should I marry both of you right now? And live happily ever after. I clearly have the two most awesome people next to me." The words spilled from her lips, wrapped in humor, but beneath the surface, deeper currents moved— wishes disguised as jokes, dreams dressed as casual commentary.

Valouna's chuckle carried layers of understanding, recognition flickering in her dark eyes. "No way I'm that easy, Samee, my luv! You're going to need more than two dates with me before you can ask me to marry you both."

For a split second, no one laughed.

The words hung there longer than they should have.

Samee felt it the moment she said it—that strange shift in the air, like something unspoken had just been exposed.

John's smile lingered, but it wasn't as easy as before.

And Valou… Valou didn't look away.

She held Samee's gaze just a little too long.

Not confused.

Not amused.

Just… aware.

Then, just as quickly, the moment passed.

John's smile wavered like candlelight in a draft. His gaze shifted to Samee, reading the subtle signs of her displacement, the way her shoulders had drawn inward. He couldn't deny the truth humming between his ribs—his connection with Valouna flowed like water finding its natural course. At the same time, his attraction to Samee burned with a different kind of fire, physical and consuming but somehow less intellectually complete.

"Yeah, remember the horror movie we saw last week on ZOELY? You were way braver than I was." His attempt to bridge the gap between them carried genuine warmth, a lifeline thrown across the growing distance.

Samee's smirk returned, gratitude and mischief dancing across her features as she leaned forward to press her lips to his. The kiss tasted of wine and reconciliation. As she turns to Valou with a smile on her face. "You want a kiss, too."

Valou accidently touch Samee on her little breast, trying to stop Samee from kissing her. Samee pretended to be outrage. "Baby, you see Valou touching my breast, trying to flirt with me."

John's chuckle emerged awkwardly, caught between amusement and uncertainty. Valouna watched the interaction with eyes that held secrets, her smile mysterious as moonlight on water. The irony wasn't lost on her—John embodied precisely the type of man who typically caught her attention, while Samee's usual preferences ran toward an entirely different archetype. Time had shifted them both, maturity reshaping desires like rivers carving new channels through a familiar landscape.

The restaurant door exhaled them into the night's embrace. Cool air nipped at their skin as they walked hand in hand down the dimly lit street, their footsteps creating a rhythm against the concrete. Streetlights carved pools of yellow illumination while shadows stretched between them like dark fingers reaching for secrets.

Valou's mind raced with dangerous thoughts. She had finally done it—selected exactly the type of man she wouldn't mind exploring one of Samee's wild experiences with. The realization sent tremors through her soul, awakening desires she had buried beneath layers of caution and self-preservation. His cologne drifted toward her on the evening breeze, something warm and masculine with hints of cedar and spice. The scent invaded her senses, creating chaos in her carefully ordered world.

"I was thinking we should grab dessert at that cute place I see over there?" Samee's voice cut through Valou's internal storm.

Valou hesitated, her gaze finding John's face in the streetlight's glow. He smiled at her with easy warmth, and the unspoken connection between them hummed like high-voltage wires. The intensity frightened her, this sudden awakening to possibilities she had spent years avoiding.

"Uh, I think I'm going to head home. I've got an early start tomorrow." The lie slipped from her lips with practiced ease.

Samee's eyebrows rose in genuine surprise. "Really? Valou, my love, you never skip dessert. You feeling okay?"

"Yeah, well, I'm trying this new thing called 'self-control.'" Valouna's soft chuckle barely masked the turbulence beneath her composed exterior.

John's laughter joined hers, but Samee's nod carried the weight of recognition—something had shifted, though its exact nature remained elusive as morning mist.

"Alright, well, we'll catch up soon. Let's discuss your film idea further next time. I'm really glad you're coming out tonight." John's words conveyed genuine appreciation, unaware of the profound effect his simple presence had on her.

"Yeah, definitely. Night, guys." Valouna's smile felt tight across her face as she turned away from them, from the dangerous territory their triangle had begun to chart.

As her silhouette disappeared into the night's embrace, John watched her departure with thoughtful intensity. The expression didn't escape Samee's notice. Her grip on his arm tightened imperceptibly, fingers pressing against muscle and bone with subtle possession.

"My friend is pretty awesome, am I right?" Her words carried layers—pride, testing, something sharper beneath the casual observation.

John's half-smile emerged cautiously, his attempt at deflection falling short of convincing. "I don't know if I'm special now, cause... You literally went and found the male version of your best friend so you can date him."

The observation hung between them like a challenge thrown down on ancient ground. Samee's silence stretched, filling the space with unspoken acknowledgments and dangerous truths. They walked deeper into the night, but tension followed them like a hungry shadow, feeding on what remained unsaid.

Samee's condo bathed in afternoon sunlight that streamed through floor-to-ceiling windows, casting geometric patterns across the hardwood floors. The space reflected her aesthetic—clean lines, neutral colors, and carefully curated art pieces that conveyed sophistication and success. But today, the pristine environment would witness something far more primal.

John arrived carrying the weight of nervous anticipation— round two. The phrase echoed through his consciousness like a mantra, a prayer to whatever gods governed sexual performance and masculine pride. He couldn't bear to disappoint again, couldn't survive another assessment delivered with casual cruelty. Samee had become his addiction, the substance his system craved with increasing desperation. His only wish burned like fever through his veins—for his drug to become as addicted to him as he was to her.

Samee's clothes pooled on the floor like shed inhibitions. The previous evening's dinner had left her simmering with arousal, the chemistry between all three of them creating a cocktail of desire and possibility. She closed her eyes, surrendering to fantasy, imagining Valouna's presence in the room with them. The memory of their first encounter blazed through her consciousness like wildfire.

College. The book club meeting. Andre Lazama sat across from them in the cramped dorm room, his thick glasses reflecting fluorescent light as he pontificated about literature's power to transport readers beyond their mundane existence. Valou had watched him with undisguised fascination, her attraction evident as sunrise and Samee knew it. And all she wanted to do, was to help her friend find happiness.

"Can your stupid books be as sweet as a kiss from Valouna?" Samee's boldness had always been her trademark, the quality that pushed boundaries and shattered careful facades.

Andre blushed furiously, adjusting his glasses with trembling fingers. "It depends on who the writer is. Some writers are so masterful at describing a scene. You would swear up and down you were present in the moment."

"Valou, my luv, kiss him." The words had tumbled from Samee's lips with reckless abandon.

Valouna froze, stunned by the request. Her paralysis emboldened Samee further. "You forgot how to kiss a person?" Without waiting for a response, Samee had turned to Valou, her lips finding her friends in what she intended as a friendly demonstration.

But the kiss ignited something neither had anticipated. Fire raced through their veins, awakening desires they couldn't name or control. They couldn't stop themselves if they had wanted to. Both women were doing a naked dance if front of Andre. The type of dance that's as old as ancient times. Valou's very large and luscious grapefruit size breast had place Andre in a trance; he became a breast-man that day. A forgotten observer, his fantasies shifting toward Valouna's generous curves as the two women discovered territories they had never dared explore.

Andre and Valouna dated briefly afterward, but the relationship crumbled under the weight of her secret—her undying love for Samee. This connection haunted every subsequent encounter, every attempt to recreate the magic of those stolen moments.

Now, lying beneath John's careful ministrations, Samee grappled with the same demons. His performance had improved dramatically, his technique refined by determination and genuine desire. When their eyes met in the aftermath, she read his desperate hope, his need for validation and confirmation of his worth.

Not wanting to lie or wound him, she pressed her lips to his with tender honesty. "This was the closest I've ever been."

Morning light filtered through the bedroom's sheer curtains as Samee emerged holding two tickets like playing cards in a high-stakes game. John stirred from sleep, consciousness returning slowly as he focused on her silhouette against the windows.

"Hey, babe, I totally forgot I had these." She waved the tickets with casual nonchalance.

"Tickets to what?" John's voice carried the rough edges of recent sleep.

"It's the play Valou's been dying to see. 'Maybe Happy Ending.' I got them from the modeling house where I did yesterday's event. They are nonrefundable. So, you have to take Valou with you."

"Seriously? Why can't you come with me?" Confusion clouded his features as pieces of a puzzle he couldn't quite solve shifted in his mind.

"I'm flying to Paris today for a photoshoot and a fashion show. I won't be in town for the next seven days." She handed him the tickets, her smile carrying enigmatic undercurrents.

"I'm sure you guys could have a Happy Ending night out without me."

John stared at the tickets as if they might reveal hidden messages written in invisible ink. Was this a loyalty test? Some elaborate examination of his character and commitment? The uncertainty gnawed at him like hunger.

"Wait, what? Me and Valou... just, the two of us?"

"Yeah, why not? It's a play. You're not going to actually give her a Happy Ending, unless I'm there to watch." Samee's kiss landed on his lips with calculated casualness, but tension threaded through her voice like wire through silk.

John's confusion deepened. Was she joking or deadly serious? The line between humor and invitation blurred beyond recognition.

"Are you sure you're okay with this?"

"Of course! You two are my two favorite people in the world. It would bring me joy to see you guys closer." Her smile radiated warmth, but shadows moved beneath the surface like fish in murky water.

John's uncertainty warred with acceptance. He nodded, sliding the tickets into his pocket with the careful precision of someone handling volatile materials.

"Alright... if you're sure."

Samee's final kiss brushed his cheek like a butterfly's wing. "Have fun. I'll be with you both in spirit."

As her footsteps faded down the hallway, John remained motionless, contemplating the bizarre parameters of the situation. He threw aside the bed sheets, staring down at himself with grim amusement.

"This girl doesn't know who I am. The old me would fuck her best friend. And send her crying back to her arms. Damn, I'm getting soft."

The theater's marquee blazed against the night sky like a beacon drawing moths to their destruction, its electric bulbs pulsing with the rhythm of a heartbeat against the velvet darkness. "Maybe Happy Ending" glowed in brilliant letters above the crowd of theatergoers streaming through the ornate entrance—a title that seemed to mock the very uncertainty that had brought John and Valou to this sidewalk, to this moment, to this precipice they hadn't quite acknowledged they were standing on.

John adjusted his collar for the third time in as many minutes, one of John's many habits Samee found endearing. If she were here right now, she would kiss him until his nerves transformed, making him cool, calm, and collected. But Valouna didn't seem to notice—or if she did, she didn't mind. She stood beside him beneath the electric proclamation, her breath visible in small puffs against the cool evening air, her attention focused on the theater's facade with the kind of wonder he rarely saw in adults.

Streetlights flickered to life as dusk gave way to darkness, their amber glow casting the sidewalk in warm pools of illumination. Couples and groups hurried past them toward the evening's entertainment, wrapped in scarves and linked arm in arm, their voices carrying fragments of anticipation and excitement. The city's energy hummed around them like a living thing—car engines purring through the theater district, distant music spilling from restaurant doorways, fragments of conversation in half a dozen languages blending into the urban symphony that never quite reached silence.

A homeless man sat in the doorway of a closed boutique across the street, his weathered face catching the theater's reflected light as he watched the parade of well-dressed patrons. John found himself wondering about the distance between that doorway and where he stood, about the arbitrary nature of comfort and suffering, about whether happiness was something you earned or something that simply happened to you while you were making other plans.

"You sure Samee was okay with this? I'm awkward." Valouna's smile couldn't quite mask her discomfort, the way her fingers worried the hem of her dress—a vintage piece she'd found at a consignment shop in Brooklyn, navy blue with tiny silver threads that caught the light when she moved.

The question hung between them like a physical presence. John had rehearsed his answer during the subway ride here, had practiced the casual confidence he wanted to project. But now, looking at Valouna's face—really looking at it, noting the way her eyebrows drew together when she was uncertain, the small scar above her left eyebrow from a childhood accident she'd never told him about—the rehearsed words felt inadequate.

"I kid you not. She insisted." John's nod carried conviction, though uncertainty still lingered in his eyes like storm clouds on distant horizons. The truth was more complicated, of course. Samee had insisted, but her insistence had felt like a test he didn't understand the parameters of. "She's the one who gave me the tickets and immediately suggested I take you instead. "She'd appreciate it more than I would, Samee told me. As she prepared for a week-long modeling event and photo shoots, her manager booked her in the South of France. Not looking up from her laptop, she was excited for the work opportunity ahead of her." The dismissal had stung, but her logic was sound—Valouna did love theater, had studied it in college before life redirected her toward more practical pursuits.

What John didn't mention was the way Samee's eyes had tracked his reaction when she made the suggestion, as if she were conducting an experiment and he was the unwitting subject. He didn't mention the strange smile that had played at the corners of her mouth when he'd agreed, or the way she'd kissed him goodbye that morning—too brief, too casual, like she was already somewhere else entirely.

They shared a glance heavy with unspoken recognition, two people suddenly aware that the ground beneath their feet wasn't as solid as they'd assumed. The situation defied conventional boundaries—a man taking his girlfriend's best friend to a romantic musical while said girlfriend is in a whole different country. Neither wanted to examine it too closely, to pull at the threads that might unravel something they weren't prepared to see.

Valouna's soft laughter carried notes of surrender and anticipation, a sound like wind chimes in a gentle breeze. "Well, I'm not going to complain. I've been dying to see this play." Her enthusiasm was genuine, uncomplicated in a way that made John's chest tighten with something he couldn't quite name. Samee is a girly girl who plays the wife role almost to perfection. But Valou would give you more in-depth conversations instead of the generic Did you eat for the day?"

The realization hit him like a minor betrayal—not of Samee, but of himself. He was comparing them, measuring one woman's joy against another's careful reserve. The thought made him feel guilty and exhilarated in equal measure.

"Same here. It's been forever since I've been to a Broadway show." John's grin fed off her excitement, her enthusiasm infectious as laughter. The last show had been with Samee, four months ago—a gritty drama about urban decay that she'd chosen because a critic in the Times had called it "unflinchingly honest." They'd sat through two and a half hours of relentless bleakness, and afterwards, over dinner, her excitement was more prevalent for the food we ordered than the show we had just watched. She dissected every bite she placed in her mouth. Claiming she'll duplicate this evening dinner selection, the next time I come over to her house. I smiled at her that day, thinking to myself, how can I be this lucky.

A group of teenagers pushed past them toward the theater entrance, their voices bright with the kind of unselfconscious happiness that comes before life teaches you to question every moment of joy. One of them—a girl with purple streaks in her hair and paint-stained fingers—caught Valouna's eye and grinned.

"Great dress," the girl called out as her friends pulled her along.

Valouna's face lit up with the compliment, but she didn't twirl. She simply said, "Thank you!" her voice carrying genuine pleasure at the stranger's kindness.

John watched this exchange with something that felt dangerously close to wonder. Samee would have twirled and made her silver threads in her dress catch the lights like stars might have even said thank you, but she would have definitely put on a show with obvious delight. There was something guarded about Valou that both attracted and terrified him— not wanting a willingness to be seen, to no one but me. Two beautiful models with two different mindsets, yet John's secret hunger for both feels like Siamese twins.

The theater's doors beckoned with their promise of dimmed lights and shared darkness, of two hours of scripted drama to distract them from the unscripted complications of their own lives. The ornate brass handles had been polished until they gleamed, and through the glass doors, they could see the lobby's opulent interior: marble floors, crystal chandeliers, and walls lined with photographs of stars from decades past who had graced this same stage.

"Ready?" John asked, though he wasn't sure if he was asking about the play or something else entirely.

Valouna nodded, her hand brushing his arm as they moved toward the entrance together—two people balanced on the edge of choices that would reshape everything they thought they understood about desire, loyalty, and the dangerous territories of the heart. The touch was brief, accidental, but it sent electricity through his entire nervous system, a reminder that some forces couldn't be controlled or planned for.

As they approached the doors, John caught their reflection in the glass—a man and woman who looked, to any observer, like a couple heading out for an evening of entertainment. The image was both accurate and completely false, and the contradiction made him feel like he was living in two different stories simultaneously.

Behind them, the city pulsed with its endless rhythms of connection and separation, of people finding each other and losing each other, only to meet again in the infinite dance of urban life. Above them, the marquee continued its electric proclamation: "Maybe Happy Ending"—three words that contained multitudes of possibility and doubt, promise and warning, hope and heartbreak, all blazing against the darkness like a question waiting to be answered.

CHAPTER 7
SILENT LONGINGS

The theater's velvet seats embraced John and Valou as darkness descended around them. Whispered conversations died to murmurs, programs rustled like autumn leaves, and the stage lights blazed to life. John shifted slightly, his shoulder brushing against Valouna's cashmere sweater. She smelled of jasmine and something warmer—vanilla, perhaps, or sandalwood.

The actors moved across the stage with practiced grace, their voices carrying into the hushed auditorium. Valouna leaned forward, captivated, her dark eyes reflecting the stage lights. When the leading man delivered a particularly witty line, she pressed her hand to her mouth to stifle a laugh, and John found himself watching her instead of the performance.

Their hands collided as they both reached for the program between them. The contact lasted three heartbeats—long enough for John to register the softness of her skin, the slight tremor in her fingers. She withdrew first, tucking a strand of hair behind her ear, and they both pretended to study the stage with renewed interest.

But the absence of her touch didn't feel like relief.

It felt like something had been taken away too soon.

John kept his eyes on the stage, but his mind refused to follow the dialogue. He was aware of her now in a way he hadn't been before-every slight movement, every shift in her posture, every breath she took beside him.

And Valou felt it too. Her hand rested in her lap, but her fingers hadn't quite relaxed.

Not completely, Not yet. As if they still remembered him.

But the damage was done. The air between them hummed with unspoken possibility.

Cool night air hit them as they emerged from the theater onto the bustling sidewalk. Couples streamed past, some debating the play's merits, others walking in companionable silence. Valouna's heels clicked against the pavement as she turned to John, her face animated.

"The show was so amazing. Do you really think love can be found in the most unexpected places?"

John grinned, stuffing his hands into his coat pockets. The question struck deeper than she probably intended. "Yeah, I think so… I wasn't expecting it to be so immersive. I thought plays were supposed to be… well, kind of slow."

Valouna nudged him with her elbow, the gesture playful and familiar. "See? I told you! You just needed to give it a shot."

Their laughter mingled with the city's symphony—car horns, distant music, the shuffle of a hundred footsteps. John stole glances at her as they walked, noting how her enthusiasm transformed her entire face.

A small café appeared ahead, its windows glowing amber against the dark street. Valou slowed, her smile turning tentative.

"This place looks quaint, and the night's still young. Do you mind if we stop in for a few?"

John hesitated. Samee's face flickered through his mind— her trust, it's a commodity he refuses to lose. But Valou stood before him, real and present, and the pull was undeniable.

"Yeah, why not?"

Steam rose from their coffee cups in lazy spirals. The café wrapped around them like a cocoon, dim lighting casting intimate shadows across their small table. Only a handful of other patrons occupied the space—

a couple sharing dessert in the corner, an elderly man reading behind wire-rimmed glasses.

"I've been thinking of switching careers," John admitted, surprising himself with the confession. "I mean, I like my job, but it's not exactly fulfilling, you know?"

Valou cradled her mug between her palms, considering his words. "I get that. It's tough to walk away from stability, though. But sometimes, you just need to take the leap."

Their conversation deepened as the evening wore on. Dreams shared tentatively, fears acknowledged with gentle understanding. John watched Valouna's expressions shift like the weather—thoughtful, amused, concerned. When she smiled, really smiled, it transformed her entire face.

"I'm really glad we did this, John. It's nice... getting to know you like this."

Her voice carried a softness he hadn't heard before. John nodded, his voice quieter than usual. "Yeah, me too."

The moment stretched between them, fragile and charged. Neither moved to break it.

The walk to Valouna's mother's three-family brownstone building in Harlem passed too quickly. They lingered on the sidewalk, neither quite ready to end the evening. The building's entrance light cast everything in harsh relief—the crack in the concrete, the nervous flutter of Valouna's hands, the uncertainty in John's stance.

"Thanks for tonight, John. I had a really great time. If things were different... You would've definitely gotten some happy ending tonight."

The words hung in the air. Valouna's eyes widened as if she couldn't believe she'd spoken them aloud.

"I'm so sorry, I can't believe I said that."

John's smile came more easily than expected. "I'm sorry too, I was thinking the same thing."

"No, no, no… let's not start anything we can't finish."

"What I meant to say was… I had a great time with you, and I hope we can do it again sometime soon."

Valou's gaze dropped to the pavement, then lifted to meet his again. Her expression softened, becoming almost vulnerable. "Yeah. We should."

She moved closer, and John caught her scent again— jasmine and warmth and something uniquely her. The kiss landed on his cheek, soft and brief, but she lingered afterward. For a heartbeat, maybe two, her face remained close to his. Her breath whispered against his skin.

The effort it took her to step away was visible—a tightening around her eyes, a quick inhale. She turned and hurried toward her building's entrance without looking back, leaving John standing on the empty sidewalk with the phantom touch of her lips burning against his cheek.

He remained there long after her door closed, his mind a tangle of want and guilt and possibility.

The week passed in a blur of stolen moments. Museums, coffee shops, long walks through Central Park—each day brought them closer, the connection strengthening like metal under heat. John told himself they were friends, nothing more.

But friendship didn't explain the way his pulse quickened when she laughed, or how her absence left the day feeling incomplete.

On the fourth day, at MoMA, their carefully constructed bubble burst.

John stood before a Pollock painting, trying to decipher meaning in the chaos of paint splatters, when a familiar voice cut through the gallery's hushed atmosphere.

"Since when do you like going to museums?"

He turned to find Jennifer approaching, her arm linked still with Tom's. Five years had treated her well—her hair was shorter, more expensive-looking, and her clothes spoke of a comfortable life. But her eyes held the same sharp intelligence that had first drawn him to her. "What are you talking about? I love the arts. You're the one who used to make excuses on why you couldn't come."

"Oh yeah, you're right. But now, since I found a man with the patience of a saint, who knows how to explain each art piece in a very interesting way, I love it now too." Jennifer replied, glancing at her companion with obvious affection.

Before John could respond, Valouna appeared at his side, sliding her arm around his waist with practiced ease. She was wearing a form-fitting black dress that highlighted every curve, her confidence radiating like heat.

"Baby, you have to see this next piece—it's incredibly beautiful. Looking at it makes me want to do some nasty things to you, with you, for you; however, you want it." Her voice carried a sultry promise before she pretended, she just now noticing Jennifer and her companion. "Oh, hi… I didn't see you guys there. I'm Samaya, John's fiancée, and you two are?" Jennifer's composure cracked. "I was married to him for seven years and divorced for five. I never knew he was into black women."

Valouna's smile turned predatory. "John is into young, sexy, beautiful women. The fact that my skin's been kissed by the sun is his added bonus."

"Oh, of course," Jennifer managed, her voice tight.

The man beside her stepped forward, extending his hand.

"My man John… wow… way to bounce back. Congratulations."

"Let's go, Tom," Jennifer's voice cut through the gallery like a whip.

Tom's handshake was firm, his expression genuinely apologetic. "I'm sorry about how things went down. I was divorced, and Jennifer was an escape from my pain. I'm really glad you found happiness again."

"Tom, I said, let's go!" Jennifer's second command brooked no argument.

As they disappeared into the crowd, Valouna turned to John with triumph blazing in her eyes. The performance had been flawless, but more than that—it had felt real. Too real.

From that moment, they became inseparable. The fiancée charade gave them permission to touch, to hold hands, to kiss in public. They took photos like honeymooners, each image capturing genuine joy and desire. For three perfect days, they lived in their created reality.

But reality has a way of intruding.

Samee was coming home tomorrow.

The bar pulsed with Friday night energy. Bodies pressed together on the dance floor, voices rose above the thundering bass, and empty shot glasses accumulated on their high table like trophies. John sat between Samee and Valou, the alcohol making the world soft around the edges.

"You guys seriously dragged me into this!" John's words slurred slightly as he gestured toward the collection of empty glasses. "I'm not even sure how I'm still standing!"

Samee's hand found his arm, her grip possessive yet playful. "Oh, please. You're loving it."

Valou threw back another shot, the tequila burning a familiar path down her throat. "John's a trooper. Did he tell you how we met his ex and I pretended to be you?"

Samee's face lit up with curiosity. "He forgot to mention it. What happened?"

"Well, this bitch had a whole new man next to her but was still catching feelings because she saw her ex with little me— at the prime of my existence. Body curvy, booty delicious, skin glowing like Queen Nefertiti herself." Valouna's voice took on a mocking tone. "This bitch looked at me and said, 'I was with John for twenty years, I never knew he liked black women.' Bitch, I am a model with breasts like two Haitian mangos squeezing together. And all you can see is that I'm a black woman?"

As Valouna reenacted the story, she leaned into John, showing Samee how well of an actress she was, as her lips found his in a kiss that started as a performance but lingered with genuine heat. Samee got so excited that her left hand slipped to John's pants zipper, as she touched it up and down boldly and encouragingly.

The three of them laughed, but something fundamental had shifted. When John and Valouna's eyes met across the small table, the connection was electric, undeniable. Samee witnessed it all, her smile never wavering as she raised her glass.

"To us! The best… throuple ever!"

The word hung in the air like a challenge. They clinked glasses, and Samee rose to plant a soft kiss on Valouna's lips. The contact sent memory spiraling through Valouna's mind— late nights tangled in sheets, whispered promises, the particular way Samee's touch could ignite her entire body.

The flashback hit her like a physical blow: lying in bed after lovemaking, her heart raw and exposed.

Flashback the last time they made love to each other.

"Why can't we try to make us work… instead of you keep bringing new money with no class in our bed?"

Samee's response had been as gentle as it was devastating: "Valou, my love, we talked about this already. I need dick too.

Or else one day I'll cheat on you."

After the Bar

John's apartment welcomed them with familiar warmth, the soft glow of the lamp he'd left on casting everything in golden relief. They stumbled through the door in a tangle of limbs and laughter, the night's accumulated tension finally finding release in movement and sound. Shoes kicked off carelessly landed in a scattered constellation across the hardwood—Valouna's vintage heels, John's leather oxfords, Samee's ankle boots that had cost more than most people's rent. Inhibitions seemed to have been left somewhere between the bar and the taxi ride home, abandoned like breadcrumbs on a trail they couldn't retrace.

"Why does your couch feel like a cloud?" Samee mumbled now, sinking into the cushions with the boneless grace of someone who'd had just enough to drink to feel weightless. "Seriously… I could live here."

The couch had been an extravagance; a piece John had bought during a particularly successful quarter at work. Italian leather, custom-made, ridiculously expensive. Samee had initially criticized it as an unnecessary luxury, but she'd spent countless evenings curled up on it, reading or working on her laptop, gradually claiming it as her territory.

Valou stretched out beside her, head tilted back, dark hair spilling over the armrest like water over stone. "It's so comfortable…" Her voice carried the dreamy quality of someone floating between consciousness and sleep, between intention and accident.

John perched on the edge, torn between concern and anticipation. The alcohol buzzed through his system like electricity through copper wire, but awareness remained sharp beneath the haze. He could feel the weight of the moment, the sense that they were balanced on the edge of something that would change everything. "You guys... maybe we should get some water or—"

The words died in his throat as Samee's arms circled his neck, pulling him down between them with gentle but insistent pressure. Her laugh was rich and uninhibited, but underneath lay something more serious, more calculated. It was the laugh of someone who had made a decision and was now committed to seeing it through, consequences be damned.

Valouna's face was suddenly inches from his, close enough that he could count her eyelashes, see the flecks of gold in her brown eyes that reminded him of amber with insects trapped inside—beautiful and precious and somehow dangerous. Her pupils were dilated, whether from alcohol or something else, he couldn't tell. Her lips were slightly parted, and he could feel her breath against his skin, warm and sweet with the lingering taste of the wine they'd shared.

"We're all best friends, right?" Samee's voice carried a teasing lilt as she pulled Valou into their embrace, creating a triangle of limbs and heat and possibility. Her fingers traced patterns on both their arms, claiming them, marking territory, establishing ownership in a way that felt both generous and possessive.

The tension was palpable now, charged with possibility and danger like the air before a thunderstorm. John and Valou remained frozen, neither pulling away nor moving closer, caught in the gravitational pull of something they'd both been denying for weeks. John could feel his heart beating against his ribs, could hear the sound of his own breathing, could smell the mixture of perfume and alcohol and something else— something that belonged to all three of them together.

Valouna's eyes searched his face, looking for permission, for warning, for some sign of what he wanted. Her hand had somehow found its way to his chest, her palm flat against his heart, and he wondered if she could feel how fast it was beating, if she understood the war being fought between his desire and his conscience.

Samee's breath was warm against John's ear when she whispered, "You'll never need my permission to kiss her. Her lips haunt my dreams."

The words hit him like a physical blow, recontextualizing everything he thought he understood about their relationship, about the dynamics that had been building for months. Samee had been watching, had been thinking about this, had been planning something he couldn't quite grasp. The revelation was intoxicating and terrifying in equal measure.

Permission granted, barriers dissolved like sugar in water.

John and Valouna came together like magnets, finding true north, like two parts of a whole that had been artificially separated. The kiss was everything their earlier restraint had denied—hungry, desperate, charged with weeks of unspoken desire and careful distance. Her hands fisted in his shirt, pulling him closer, while his fingers tangled in her hair, marveling at its softness, at the way it caught the light from the lamp.

The world narrowed to the taste of her mouth—wine and something sweeter, something that was purely her. She made a soft sound against his lips, part surprise, part surrender, and he felt something fundamental shift inside him, like tectonic plates finding a new configuration. This was what he'd been denying himself, what he'd been afraid to want, what he'd been pretending didn't exist in the spaces between words and glances.

Samee watched for long moments, her own breathing shallow, her eyes dark with something that might have been arousal or might have been something else entirely. Her hand traced patterns on both their backs, connecting them, claiming them, making them part of something larger than themselves. When she finally joined them in the tangle of limbs and heat and possibility, it felt like the completion of a circuit that had been building charge for months.

Her lips found John's neck, then Valouna's shoulder, creating a chain of connection that made all three of them gasp. The boundaries between them began to dissolve—whose hand was where, whose breath was whose, whose desire was driving the moment forward. They moved together like dancers who had rehearsed this choreography in dreams, each touch leading naturally to the next, each kiss deepening the spell they were weaving around themselves.

The night stretched ahead, full of choices that would reshape everything they thought they understood about love, desire, and the complex geography of the human heart. Outside, the city continued its endless rhythms, but inside John's apartment, time seemed to slow and thicken, each moment expanding to contain multitudes of sensation and possibility.

CHAPTER 8
WALLS FALLING

The bedroom door closed with a soft click behind them, the sound as final as a judge's gavel, sealing the three of them in their private universe where the rules of the outside world no longer applied. The room was dimly lit by the bedside lamp John had forgotten to turn off that morning, casting everything in warm amber tones that made their skin look like it had been painted by candlelight. The space felt both intimate and vast—intimate because of what they were about to share, vast because they were crossing into uncharted territory where maps meant nothing and only instinct could guide them.

Samee tumbled onto the bed first, her laughter breathless and intoxicating, a sound that seemed to bubble up from some deep well of joy and mischief. The mattress bounced slightly under her weight, and she spread her arms wide as if claiming the space, as if declaring herself queen of this new realm they were creating. Her dress had ridden up, revealing the long line of her thighs, and John found himself staring, remembering all the times he'd imagined this moment and how the reality was both exactly what he'd expected and nothing like he'd prepared for.

She pulled John down with her, her fingers tangling in his shirt, her grip insistent but playful. He let himself fall, let gravity and desire carry him into her embrace, feeling the softness of the sheets beneath them and the warmth of her body against his. Valou followed, drawn by forces that seemed beyond conscious choice—gravity, desire, and the magnetic pull of inevitable collision.

For a moment, they lay there in a triangle of possibility, each aware of the others' breathing, each feeling the weight of the decision they'd made and the decisions they were about to make. John could smell Samee's perfume mixed with the wine on her breath, could feel Valou's hand trembling slightly where it rested on his arm. The air between them felt charged, electric, as if they were about to conduct some dangerous experiment with the very nature of intimacy itself.

What happened next unfolded with the slow-motion clarity of dreams. For a moment… no one moved.

Samee's laughter faded into something quieter, more intentional, and John felt it first—the shift. This wasn't just play anymore, not just chemistry. This was a line, and once crossed, there would be no returning to who they had been before. He looked at Valou really looked at her, not as Samee's friend, not as the woman he had been trying not to want, but as someone standing in the same moment, making the same choice. Valou's breath caught slightly; she knew it too. Samee didn't speak-she didn't have to because the decision had already been made, not with words,

But with silence and the urgent hunger of bodies that had been denied for too long. Time seemed to stretch and compress simultaneously, each second containing hours of sensation while minutes passed like heartbeats. Hands explored territories previously forbidden, fingers tracing maps of skin that had been glimpsed but never touched, mouths discovering new territories of pleasure that tasted of salt and wine and something indefinably sweet.

The careful boundaries they'd maintained for months—the space between friends, the distance between desire and action, the walls between what was imagined and what was real— dissolved like sugar in rain, leaving nothing but the essential truth of their attraction to each other.

Samee's fingers traced the strong line of John's jaw with reverent precision, as if she were memorizing the angle of bone beneath skin, the slight roughness of stubble that had grown since morning. Her touch was gentle but possessive, claiming him in a way that made his breath catch. Then her hand moved to thread through Valouna's dark hair, the strands slipping between her fingers like silk, drawing them together in a kiss that tasted of tequila and promise and the salt of tears that hadn't yet been shed.

John watched for a moment, transfixed by the sight of the two women he cared about most in the world discovering each other, their lips meeting with tentative curiosity that quickly deepened into something more urgent. Valou's eyes fluttered closed, and she made a soft sound of surprise and pleasure that went straight through him like lightning. Samee's free hand found his chest, pulling him closer, making him part of this moment, this discovery, this beautiful transgression.

John's hands found the curve of Valou's hip, marveling at the way she fit perfectly against his palm, the way her body seemed designed to be touched by him. His other hand discovered the softness of Samee's thigh, the skin warm and smooth and familiar yet somehow new in this context. The world contracted to touch and heat and the symphony of whispered names, each syllable carrying weight and meaning and promises they might not be able to keep.

Valouna's skin gleamed like burnished copper in the dim light, her body responding to every caress with liquid grace that made John think of dancers and rivers and things that moved with natural beauty. She arched into their touches, her own hands exploring with growing confidence, discovering the planes of John's chest, the curve of Samee's waist, the geography of pleasure that mapped itself across all three of them.

Samee moved between them like a conductor orchestrating desire, her elegant frame containing enough passion to ignite stars. She seemed to know exactly what each of them needed, where to touch, how to guide them deeper into this shared experience. Her lips found the hollow of John's throat, then the slope of Valouna's shoulder, creating chains of connection that bound them all together in ways that transcended the merely physical.

John lost himself in the sensation of being wanted—truly wanted—by two women who consumed him completely.

Every nerve ending felt alive, hypersensitive to the slightest touch, the softest breath. He had spent so many nights imagining something like this, but the reality overwhelmed his fantasies, left them looking pale and incomplete by comparison. This was really skin against real skin, real breath mingling with real breath, real hearts beating in synchrony with real desire.

They moved together in an ancient rhythm, three souls seeking connection in the most primal way possible. There was awkwardness at first—elbows bumping, uncertain positioning, nervous laughter that broke the tension and made them remember they were friends as well as lovers. But gradually they found their flow, their own unique choreography that belonged to no one else in the world.

The night stretched endlessly, filled with discoveries and surrenders, with moments of tenderness interwoven with raw need. They explored each other with the patience of archaeologists and the urgency of the drowning, cataloging every gasp and shiver, every way they could make each other feel alive. Sometimes they moved as one unit, a single organism of desire. Sometimes they paired off, creating intimate duets while the third watched with appreciation and anticipation for their turn.

John discovered that Valouna's most sensitive spot was just below her left ear, and that the sound she made when he kissed her there was like music. He learned that Samee liked to be held afterward, needed the reassurance of gentle touches and whispered words. Valouna found that John's shoulders were broader than they looked, that he tasted like salt and something indefinably him.

When exhaustion finally claimed them, they collapsed in a tangle of limbs and satisfaction, their breathing gradually synchronizing as sleep pulled them under. John found himself in the middle, Samee curled against his left side, her head on his chest, her dark hair spread across his skin like spilled ink. Valouna pressed against his right, her arm thrown across his waist, her face peaceful in sleep.

He lay there for a long time, listening to their breathing, feeling the weight of their bodies against his, trying to process what had just happened. The room smelled like sex and perfume and something else— something that might have been happiness or might have been the beginning of heartbreak. Through the window, he could see the first hints of dawn creeping across the sky, and he knew that when the sun rose fully, they would have to face what they had done, what they had become, what it meant for the future they had been building separately.

But for now, in the quiet darkness, with two women he loved in different ways breathing softly against him, John allowed himself to feel complete in a way he never had before. The night had given them something precious and dangerous, something that would either destroy them, transform them, or both. Whatever came next, they would face it together, bound by shared secrets and the knowledge that they had chosen connection over safety, love over convention, the beautiful chaos of the heart over the tidy order of a life lived within prescribed boundaries.

Outside, the city began to wake, but inside John's bedroom, three people slept the deep sleep of the transformed, their dreams tangled together like their bodies, their futures irrevocably intertwined by the choices they had made in the private universe they had created for themselves in the space between darkness and dawn.

Sunlight sliced through the floor-to-ceiling windows like golden blades, painting the bedroom in warm honey tones. John stirred first, consciousness returning in slow waves as his body registered unfamiliar weight and warmth on either side of him.

Reality crashed over him with devastating clarity.

Samee lay curled against his left side, her bubble braids spilled across his chest like silk. Valouna occupied his right, one long leg thrown over his hip, her face peaceful in sleep. The sheet barely covered their naked bodies, and John's mind raced to reconstruct the events that had led them here.

The memory arrived in fragments—laughter at the bar, stumbling home together, the moment when intention became action. His chest tightened with a cocktail of satisfaction and panic. What had they done? What did this mean?

Samee's eyes fluttered open, and she pressed her lips to his ear, her voice barely a whisper. "Baby, you did it."

The words he'd dreamed of hearing from her for months. But underneath the triumph lay something bitter—the knowledge he'd needed Valouna's presence to finally satisfy the woman he loved. The victory carried the taste of inadequacy.

Valouna remained motionless, staring at the ceiling with eyes too bright and too distant. Her expression revealed nothing, but John sensed the storm brewing beneath her calm surface. She'd never been good at sharing. Even in their moment of connection, part of her remained guarded, calculating.

Samee rose from the bed with feline grace, her body catching the morning light as she leaned over to kiss Valouna's forehead.

"Valou, my love, come take a shower with me," she whispered.

Valouna's response was automatic, rising to follow Samee toward the bathroom without a word. Their hands linked as they disappeared through the doorway, leaving John alone with his thoughts and the lingering scent of their shared intimacy.

His phone buzzed against the nightstand—a video call from his brother-in-law. John grabbed it without thinking, muscle memory overriding discretion.

His brother-in-law's grinning face filled the screen. "John, you are in luck, my brother. I'm at my dentist's office. They hired this new nurse. I showed her a picture of you, and she's dying to meet you. Her name is Margarette—she's forty-five years old. She has two grown kids, so there's no baby mama drama for you to deal with. She's right next to me right now… say hi."

The camera swiveled to reveal a woman with kind eyes and a warm smile. John's brain registered the absurdity of the situation—lying naked in bed after the most intense night of his life, being offered a blind date by his well-meaning relative.

"I'm naked, brother… I'll call you back." As John purposely showed his entire body on video, he then hung up the phone.

But Margarette had caught a glimpse of it all, and her reaction was immediate and enthusiastic. She grabbed a pen and paper with eager efficiency.

"Here's my cell phone number and my work number. So, from what you are telling me right now… this fine man is single?"

"I have to tell you my brother lives the most boring life. He's been divorced for five years, and all this time, his routine has been the same. Go to work, come home, and cry his heart out. It's so bad my wife—his sister—has to visit him every two

weeks to make sure he's okay."

His brother-in-law told no lies. This was an accurate and painful description of John's life pre-Samee existence.

"Wow… this is exactly the type of man I was looking for. You've got me blushing for a man I haven't even met yet. You know what, I'm going to give you twenty percent off this dental visit. I have to take care of my new brother-in-law."

"Oh no, please don't feel obligated to continue giving me discounts every time I come for a dental visit. But I appreciate it, my new sister-in-law."

Their laughter echoed through the phone but John had already ended the call, setting the device aside with careful deliberation. One night with Samee and Valou was like Clorox to his pain. Killing 99.9% of the sadness, he was carrying inside himself.

The weeks that followed blurred together in a montage of stolen moments and shared adventures, time moving with the fluid quality of a fever dream where reality and fantasy merged into something entirely new. The three of them became inseparable, their individual gravitational pulls combining into a single force that drew them together with magnetic inevitability. Their broken hearts—John's from years of feeling inadequate, Samee's from whatever had driven her to orchestrate that first night, Valouna's from relationships that had never quite understood her depth—found solace in the warmth they created together, healing in ways none of them had thought possible.

From the ashes of their individual failures, they constructed something new—fragile but beautiful, complicated but real, like a house of cards built in a gentle breeze that somehow refused to fall. It defied conventional wisdom, challenged societal norms, and yet it worked with a harmony that surprised even them. They developed their language of glances and touches, their rituals and rhythms, their way of moving through the world as a cohesive unit that seemed both natural and revolutionary.

Ice cream dates became a weekly tradition in Central Park, where they would spread a blanket under the ancient elms and pretend to be tourists in their city. Valouna had discovered John's weakness for mint chocolate chip and would feed him spoonfuls with a theatrical flourish, making him close his eyes and guess the flavor. At the same time, she added her embellishments—"This one has hints of summer rain and stolen kisses." Samee would capture these moments on her phone with the eye of a professional photographer, creating a private gallery of their happiness that she guarded like state secrets. She had begun to see beauty differently, to notice the way light caught in Valouna's hair or the curve of John's smile when he thought no one was watching.

The park became their sanctuary, a place where they could be themselves without explanation or apology. They would lie in the grass with their heads touching, making up stories about the clouds, sharing childhood memories and future dreams with the easy intimacy of people who had nothing left to hide from each other. Joggers would pass and smile at what they assumed was a group of close friends enjoying the afternoon, never suspecting the complex web of affection and desire that connected them.

Dancing until dawn at underground clubs became another cornerstone of their new existence. These weren't the trendy spots featured in magazines, but hidden venues in converted warehouses and abandoned buildings where the bass thrummed through their bones and sweat became their shared currency. The music was always too loud, the air thick with heat and bodies and the kind of raw energy that only emerged after midnight. On the dance floor, they moved as one organism, John's hands on Samee's hips while she pressed back against Valou, creating a chain of connection that made other dancers stop and stare.

Valou was the best dancer among them, her body moving with a fluid grace that seemed to channel the music directly from the speakers into her nervous system. She would close her eyes and let the rhythm take her, her movements becoming a form of prayer, meditation, or pure joy made manifest. John, who had always been self-conscious about dancing, found himself moving with new confidence when sandwiched between them, their energy lifting him beyond his usual inhibitions.

Valou surprised them both with her ability to lose herself in the music; this woman, who had analyzed everything, suddenly became pure instinct and movement. She would throw her head back and laugh as the bass dropped, her usual control dissolving into something wilder and more authentic. These were the moments when John loved her most—when she let herself be imperfect and just be alive. Samee and John's love gave her the confidence to be more like Samee in public.

The fashion shows were a different kind of performance, elegant affairs where John sat in the front row wearing a suit that cost more than most people's monthly rent, watching his lovers command the runway with professional grace. The first time he attended one of Samee's shows, he had been nervous, unsure of the protocol, and afraid of embarrassing her in front of industry professionals. But she had introduced him with evident pride—"This is John, my partner"—and he had seen the flicker of curiosity in people's eyes when they tried to parse the dynamics of their relationship.

Valouna had been featured in several shows that season, her striking features and natural poise making her a favorite among photographers and designers. John would watch her transform from the woman who fed him ice cream in the park into this goddess-like creature who owned the catwalk, her professional mask perfect and impenetrable. But he could see the tiny smile she reserved just for him and Samee, the almost imperceptible wink that reminded him that beneath the fantasy was someone real, someone who would come home with them afterward and complain about her aching feet while they rubbed them.

His chest would swell with pride and possession during these events, emotions that sometimes confused him with their intensity. Was he proud of their success or proud of his association with it? Did he love them for who they were or for how they made him feel about himself?

The questions would surface during quiet moments, but he learned to push them away, to focus instead on the immediate reality of their happiness.

The airplane rides were torture and ecstasy combined, long flights to fashion weeks in Paris and Milan, where the three of them would be crammed into business class seats that seemed designed to test their self-control. Samee and Valouna would bracket John in his assigned seat, their whispered suggestions about joining the mile-high club making him shift uncomfortably. At the same time, other passengers remained oblivious to the electricity crackling between them.

"The bathroom is surprisingly spacious," Valouna would murmur into his ear, her breath warm against his skin.

"I checked earlier," Samee would add from his other side, her hand finding his thigh under the airline blanket. "Very... accommodating."

John would close his eyes and try to think about quarterly reports, tax law, or anything that might calm his racing pulse. At the same time, the flight attendants offered him additional beverages, and he struggled to maintain his composure. The eight-hour flight to Paris had nearly killed him, especially when Samee had fallen asleep with her head on his shoulder and Valouna had spent the night tracing patterns on his arm with her fingertip.

They never did join the mile-high club—too risky, too public, too likely to result in federal charges—but the fantasy sustained them through countless hours of recycled air and cramped seating. Instead, they would arrive at their destinations charged with anticipation, barely making it to their hotel room before falling into each other with the desperation of people who had been separated for years rather than hours.

They moved through the city like a unit, drawing stares and whispered speculation wherever they went. Three beautiful people who seemed to glow with satisfaction and secret knowledge, who laughed too loudly and touched too easily and radiated the kind of happiness that made strangers both envious and hopeful. In restaurants, waiters would pause to watch them, trying to decode their dynamics. On the street, heads would turn as they passed, people sensing something magnetic about their connection without being able to put their finger on it.

The speculation followed them everywhere. Were they friends? Siblings? Some kind of artistic collective? The confusion in people's eyes was sometimes amusing, sometimes exhausting. John grew accustomed to the double-takes, the lingering glances, the way conversations would pause when they entered a room. If anyone disapproved, they kept their opinions to themselves—the trio radiated too much confidence and happiness to invite confrontation.

Their friends had different reactions. Some were supportive, curious, and excited by the novelty of their arrangement. Others became distant, uncomfortable with something they couldn't categorize or understand. John lost a few friendships during those weeks, relationships that couldn't survive his transformation from reliable single guy to part of something more complex. But he found he didn't miss them as much as he'd expected. When you had what he had, conventional friendships seemed somehow inadequate.

The three of them developed their own social circle, a collection of artists, models, and creative types who were more accepting of unconventional relationships. Dinner parties where everyone was beautiful and interesting and slightly damaged, where conversations ranged from philosophy to gossip to the kind of intimate confessions that only emerged after the third bottle of wine. John had never been part of such a scene before, had always been more comfortable with spreadsheets than social dynamics. Still, he found himself adapting, learning to hold his own in discussions about art, culture, and the politics of beauty.

But happiness, John was learning, could be as fragile as spun glass, beautiful to behold but liable to shatter at the slightest pressure. There were moments—fleeting but sharp—when he would catch one of them looking at him with an expression he couldn't quite read, or when he would wake up in the middle of the night to find the bed too empty, one of his lovers having retreated to the living room to stare out the window at the city lights.

There were practical complications, too. Whose apartment would they use when all three leases came up for renewal? How did you introduce your partners to family members who still believed in traditional relationship models? What happened when work required one of them to travel alone, disrupting the careful balance they had established?

And beneath it all, the question that none of them wanted to voice: Was this sustainable, or were they living in a beautiful bubble that would eventually burst under the weight of reality? The city around them pulsed with stories of relationships that had burned bright and fast, of people who had tried to build something outside conventional boundaries only to watch it collapse under external pressure or internal contradictions.

But for now, in the golden weeks after that first night, they chose to believe in the possibility of forever. They took pictures and made plans and talked about the future as if it belonged to them, as if happiness was something you could earn and keep rather than something that visited briefly before moving on to the next deserving heart.

The city spread out below them from John's seventeen floor windows, with eight million people living eight million different versions of love, loss, and hope. Somewhere out there were others like them, other people trying to rewrite the rules of the heart, other hearts refusing to be confined by convention. The thought was both comforting and terrifying—comforting because it meant they weren't alone, terrifying because it meant their story wasn't unique, wasn't guaranteed a happy ending just because they wanted one badly enough.

But in those stolen weeks between winter and spring, between their old lives and whatever came next, they allowed themselves to believe in the impossible. They chose joy over caution, connection over convention, the beautiful complexity of loving more than one person over the safe simplicity of traditional romance. And for a while—a brief, shining while— it was enough.

Two weeks into their new arrangement, John's apartment had become their sanctuary. The afternoon stretched ahead of them, promising lazy hours of contentment, when the doorbell shattered their peace.

Samee answered the door, and John heard his sister's voice—surprised but delighted—filtering through the hallway.

"I'm sorry, do I have the right apartment number?"

Samee's laughter rang clear and genuine. "Oh my gosh, you must be Laura and John's cutie patootie babies, I heard so much about. Come in, come in… please."

Jaxson's voice piped up immediately, indignant at being called a baby. "Yeah. We're not babies."

Molly's giggle followed her brother's protest, and John felt his chest tighten with affection for his niece and nephew.

"Wow, you're pretty. Are you a model?" Molly asked as they entered the living area.

"Can you tell?" Samee replied, her smile audible in her voice.

"You both are pretty," Jaxson announced, having spotted Valouna helping Laura with baby Charlie, as he lifted the infant to give his mother a moment's reprieve.

Both women smiled graciously at the compliment, but John sensed the undercurrent of tension as Laura's curiosity sharpened.

"Okay, I get it—both you ladies are incredibly beautiful, but which one of you is dating my brother?"

The question hung in the air like a blade. John, Samee, and Valouna exchanged glances, each one heavy with unspoken complexity. How could they explain their arrangement to someone who existed entirely within conventional boundaries?

Samee stepped forward, her voice carrying forced lightness. "That would be me."

The words hit Valouna like a physical blow. John watched the light dim in her eyes, saw her carefully constructed composure crack around the edges. She'd awakened from another blissful dream only to discover she was still the outsider, still the secret.

Laura's reaction was immediate and enthusiastic—a warm hug for Samee, a genuine welcome into the family. But her teasing couldn't hide her amazement at her brother's apparent upgrade in romantic prospects.

"You know my brother is old… right?"

"Yes," Samee laughed, playing her role perfectly.

"Did anybody threaten you or your family? And if you don't go out with my brother, they will hurt them? Blink if you can't talk. Tell me, please, I'll protect you."

Molly jumped into the conversation with a giggle. "My uncle is handsome. I think she's the one who's lucky 'cause any time she wants ice cream; my uncle is going to get it for her."

Everyone laughed—even Valouna managed a slight smile despite the pain radiating from her like heat from a wound.

"Molly, you are so right, baby girl. Samee is lucky to be going out with your uncle, right?"

"Yes," Molly giggled as Samee began tickling her in mock outrage.

"I'm lucky, you said? You have hurt me, my little cutie pie. I'm going to tickle you to death!"

The scene played out with warm domesticity, but John remained acutely aware of Valouna's silence. She stood at the periphery of the family circle, beautiful and isolated, watching the life she couldn't claim unfold before her eyes.

As the evening drew to a close, Laura pulled out her phone with a sisterly sense of pride.

"Let me take a picture with you so I can show it off to my friends. My brother is dating a model... Oh my, you make me gorgeous in this picture."

"Thank you," Samee replied graciously.

"Before I go, I almost forgot... John and I used to go to this charity event every year before his divorce. It happens the event is next week in Long Island... please say you'll come. And Valouna, you're welcome to come too. Don't worry about anything—I'll buy the tickets. Give me your phone."

Without waiting for permission, Laura commandeered Samee's phone with characteristic directness.

"When my brother does something stupid—'cause at some point, boys will always do something stupid—I'm giving you my number. You call me and I'll beat him up for you... But you cannot leave him. I love you, and my kids already love you. Okay... I'll call myself so I can have your number as well."

John and Samee walked Laura and the children to the elevator, sharing final goodbyes and promises to stay in touch. But when they returned to the apartment, the atmosphere had shifted dramatically.

Valouna stood by the windows, her reflection ghostlike in the darkening glass. Her shoulders held a tension that spoke of barely contained emotion.

"Am I a secret?" She asked without turning around.

"Of course not. Why would you say that? We lov—"

"So why did I feel like a secret all day today?" Valouna cut Samee off, her voice carrying the weight of accumulated hurt.

John stepped forward, attempting damage control. "I had no idea my sister was coming here with the kids."

Valouna whirled to face him, her eyes blazing. "Are you trying to take me for Booboo the Fool? 'Cause that's not what I said I'm upset about."

Samee's confusion was genuine. "I'm sorry, Valou, my love. John didn't mention me. Wait, why didn't you mention me to your sister?"

"Save it, Samee. It's not about you right now. At least you were introduced properly."

Valouna walked past them toward the bedroom, her dignity intact but her pain visible in every line of her retreating figure.

Samee turned to John, her voice carrying a note of accusation. "You should have told your sister the truth about all of us. We need her in this relationship."

The words hit John like cold water. "What are you saying, Samee? Am I the third wheel?"

"Really, John? You have two beautiful women in your bed every night, and this is what you choose to think about?"

Samee followed Valouna toward the bedroom, leaving John alone in the living room with his mounting insecurities. The glass walls that usually made him feel great expansive now seemed to mock him—transparent barriers that revealed everything while protecting nothing.

Minutes passed before sounds drifted from the bedroom. Soft murmurs escalated to sighs, then to something unmistakably intimate. John found himself drawn down the hallway, his feet moving without conscious direction.

The door stood slightly ajar, offering a view that stopped him in his tracks.

Samee and Valouna moved together with practiced intimacy, their bodies creating poetry in the lamplight. Samee's mouth traced paths across Valouna's skin. Two tall, sexy legs, a beautiful, moving masterpiece, were entangled in the shower. In the way, most heterosexual men dreamed about at least one time in their lives.. Their connection was electric, primal—a conversation conducted in touches and whispered endearments that needed no translation.

John's arousal warred with a deeper, more troubling emotion. Inadequacy crept through his veins like poison. Could he ever inspire the responses he witnessed? Could he ever know Valouna's body the way Samee obviously did?

He retreated to the living room, settling onto the couch with his phone. Pictures of their recent adventures filled the screen—three people who appeared deliriously happy, blissfully unaware of the fractures beginning to show. He tossed the device aside and rubbed his temples, trying to massage away the growing headache.

Why had Samee insisted on including Valouna in their relationship? He'd been perfectly content with Samee alone, but she'd made him understand his inadequacy in the bedroom. Now he wondered if he was becoming redundant in his own life.

Morning arrived with gentle insistence, sunlight streaming through the apartment's glass walls like liquid gold. John woke to find Valou curled against him on the couch, her breathing deep and peaceful. Sometime during the night, she'd left the bedroom to seek comfort in his arms.

The sight of Samee in the kitchen drove his doubts into temporary retreat. She wore one of his T-shirts, the fabric hanging loosely over her slender frame. Her legs went on forever, and her perfectly shaped posterior moved with unconscious sensuality as she prepared breakfast. Her breasts might be small—"little raisins," as he sometimes teasingly called them—but her face, her legs, her attitude more than compensated for any perceived deficiency.

John's frustration relocated itself to the back burner, filed away under problems for another day.

Work became John's refuge from the emotional complexity of home. His transformation was immediately apparent—a genuine smile had taken permanent residence on his face, and he found himself laughing at jokes that would have annoyed him weeks earlier. Even Tom's attempts at humor, previously grating reminders of his failed marriage, now seemed harmless enough to acknowledge.

Everyone noticed the change, but none more so than Captain Adam. The older man's eyes followed John's movements with an intensity that went beyond professional interest, though John remained oblivious to the scrutiny.

For the first time in years, John felt truly alive. But as he was rapidly learning, happiness could be as dangerous as it was intoxicating—particularly when built on foundations as shifting and uncertain as the human heart.

CHAPTER 9
SHATTERED ILLUSIONS

The morning sun carved sharp angles through the floor-to-ceiling windows of the trendy brunch spot, casting geometric patterns across weathered hardwood floors. Steam rose from ceramic mugs while the gentle hum of conversation mingled with the rhythmic hiss of the espresso machine. John settled into his chair, the metal frame creaking beneath his weight as he surveyed the artfully arranged chaos of their table—golden yolk bleeding across sourdough toast, coffee rings staining white napkins, fragments of their shared meal scattered like evidence of intimacy.

Across from him, Valouna's eyes sparked with the fervor of discovery, her hands gesturing as she spoke. The light caught the amber flecks in her dark irises, transforming her ordinary features into something luminous. Her voice carried the cadence of someone who had stumbled upon a profound truth.

"I think he must have loved a woman so deeply. He became consumed with her dreams and forgot his own. It may even have been the reason for his 5-year setback. However, within those five years, he refined his creations, such as ZOELY and ONOV. It was almost like he was possessively wanting the world to acknowledge his existence. The loneliness he must have felt, and the daily internal fights. Every failure begs him to unleash his soul. That's why he carries the name Don't Quit Life. In this universal storm, that was his shield."

John nodded, his coffee cup suspended halfway to his lips. The bitter aroma mingled with the scent of Valouna's perfume—something floral and expensive that clung to the air between them. He set the cup down with deliberate precision.

"You're not wrong, but I don't think it was that deep. The man was obsessed with a pretty face and long legs, but she was a single mother, so most of her energy was devoted to her daughter and sleep. So, falling in love with a woman who's always in crisis will leave you broke and lonely. She may even have loved him just as deeply as he loved her. The long distance, the rumors of the baby's father always calling, her generic conversation questions — "Did you eat?" — couldn't feed his hunger. And don't forget his failures. His business failures were his doing. The man was swinging at the universe, as if he were 50 Cent in the album Get Rich or Die Trying."

The words hung between them, weighted with implications neither dared acknowledge. Valouna's smile widened, her teeth catching the light as she leaned forward, drawn into their intellectual dance. The space between them seemed to compress, charged with an energy that made John's pulse quicken.

Meanwhile, Samee remained absorbed in the blue glow of her phone screen, her thumb scrolling with mechanical precision. The device cast an ethereal light across her face, highlighting the sharp angles of her cheekbones while shadows pooled beneath her eyes. She appeared oblivious to the electric current crackling between her boyfriend and best friend, lost in the digital world that demanded her constant attention.

The throaty rumble of conversation died as Samee finally registered the intimacy of their exchange. She lowered her phone with calculated slowness, the screen going black as she cleared her throat—a sound that cut through the ambient noise like a blade through silk. Her chair scraped against the floor as she shifted closer to John, her body language claiming territory.

"Do you think my love could inspire you. The way Don't Quit Life was motivated."

John's response arrived swiftly and surgically, designed to wound. "Maybe, if I post a picture of me online, would you immediately like it the way you love Jake Paul pictures?"

The words struck their target with precision. Samee's face crumpled for a microsecond before she reconstructed her composure, but the damage registered in the tightening around her eyes, the barely perceptible flinch that rippled through her shoulders.

The moment stretched taut as a wire until a familiar voice shattered the tension.

"Samee! Hey, girl!"

Janelle materialized beside their table like a force of nature—all bold patterns and confident strides, her presence filling the space with electric energy. Her outfit screamed designer labels and disposable income; each piece carefully selected to announce her success to the world. She moved with the fluid grace of someone accustomed to commanding attention, her heels clicking against the floor in a staccato rhythm.

Samee's face transformed, genuine warmth replacing the wounded expression that had been there moments before. "Janelle! Hey, what's up?"

The embrace they shared crackled with feminine energy— perfume mixing, jewelry chiming, two forces colliding in a display of friendship that felt both authentic and performative. Janelle's eyes swept across the table with predatory interest, cataloging details with the efficiency of a seasoned gossip.

"Well, look at you! Got the whole crew here, huh?"

"Yeah, this is my boyfriend, John, and—of course—you know Valou, my best friend."

Janelle's eyebrow arched with theatrical precision, her grin spreading across her face like spilled wine. She leaned toward Samee with the conspiratorial air of someone about to detonate a bomb, her voice dropping to what she imagined was a whisper but carried clearly across the small table.

"Girl, you better keep an eye on your man… cause the way Valouna is acting frisky in public with your man. I think she's ready to rename herself Uber and eat your hot sausage in her bed."

The words hit the table like shrapnel. Valouna's face flooded with crimson, the color spreading from her neck upward until even her ears burned. John's smile disintegrated, his features rearranging themselves into something unreadable. Samee's laugh emerged forced and brittle, the sound scraping against the sudden silence.

"Oh, please, Janelle. You know she'd never do that."

But Janelle was far from finished. Her hand found Valou's shoulder, fingers digging in with proprietary familiarity as she continued her assault with the enthusiasm of someone oblivious to the carnage she was creating.

"I'm just saying, Valouna, maybe it's time you found a man of your own! Forgive my bluntness, you know I can't help it. You look thirsty, girl! But you're very pretty. I'm sure if you open your eyes… you'll find there's a whole lot more men than you think, that are ready to die just to be with you."

Each word landed like a physical blow. Valouna's composure cracked, her smile becoming a grimace as she fought to maintain some semblance of dignity. The casual cruelty of the observation—delivered with such cheerful oblivion—cut deeper than any deliberate insult could have managed.

"Yeah, maybe. Thank you for the advice."

The words emerged strangled, barely audible above the ambient noise of the cafe. John shifted in his seat, the metal frame groaning under his restless movement as he witnessed Valouna's humiliation with growing discomfort.

Samee, recognizing the toxic turn of the conversation, attempted damage control with forced levity. "Alright, alright, you've had your fun. Don't listen to her, Valou. She's just being Janelle."

"You know me, girl! Anyway, I gotta run. But we should catch up soon, okay?"

"Definitely. Let's do that."

Janelle's departure left behind a wake of awkwardness that settled over the table like smoke. The easy intimacy of moments before had evaporated, replaced by a tension so thick it seemed to press against their skin. Valouna sat straighter, her spine rigid as she avoided eye contact with both of them.

"Actually, I think I'm not feeling too well. I'm going to head out."

The announcement struck with the finality of a gavel. Both John and Samee turned toward her with matching expressions of concern, but Valouna was already in motion, her purse clutched against her chest like armor.

"Please don't start. Janelle is definitely not one of those people we want in our business. She gossips too much about everybody."

But Valouna was beyond consolation. She shook her head with violent determination, her chair scraping against the floor as she stood. The forced smile she managed looked more like a snarl.

"Yeah, I'm fine. I just... I need some air."

John rose halfway from his seat, his concern overriding the awkwardness between them. The words emerged carefully, as if he were navigating a minefield.

"Don't forget, I'm picking you both for my sister's charity event tomorrow."

The reminder hung in the air like a challenge. John's apprehension was palpable—too many unresolved tensions, too many unspoken truths threatening to surface at an event where appearances mattered more than authenticity. They weren't ready for such public exposure.

"Really… you both really want me there?"

The question carried layers of meaning, each word weighted with hurt and hope in equal measure. Without waiting for an answer, Valouna turned and walked toward the exit, her heels clicking a sharp rhythm against the floor. John's wallet appeared in his hands with practiced efficiency as he settled their bill, his eyes tracking Valouna's retreat with obvious worry.

Samee pushed through the cafe's glass door, her heels striking the concrete sidewalk in urgent pursuit. The cool morning air hit them both like a slap, sharp and cleansing after the stifling atmosphere they'd left behind. She caught Valouna's arm with gentle insistence, and despite everything, Valouna managed that same brittle smile—the universal signal of women everywhere that everything was decidedly not okay.

They walked in silence through the streets of Harlem, John trailing behind like a reluctant shadow. The city moved around them with its usual indifference—cars honking, pedestrians hurrying past, the urban symphony continuing regardless of their personal drama. The walk gave them all the time to process what had happened, but it also allowed the wounds to fester.

Valouna's mother's brownstone rose before them like a sanctuary, its recently renovated facade gleaming in the morning light. Her mother is never home lately. She spends most of her time on cruise lines and her other house back in Haiti. The open floor concept welcomed them with minimalist elegance—exposed brick walls, polished concrete floors, and furniture that spoke of expensive taste and careful curation. Soul music drifted from hidden speakers, the bass line thrumming through the floorboards like a heartbeat.

They settled onto the leather sectional, the music providing a buffer against the awkwardness that had followed them home. John's intentions became clear as his hands began their familiar exploration, seeking comfort in physical connection. But Valouna wasn't receptive—her body language screamed rejection even as she tried to be polite about her refusal.

Irritation flickered across her features as she stood abruptly, her movements sharp with barely contained emotion. "I'm going to take a shower before going to sleep."

The water started running moments later, the sound of pipes groaning through the walls. John turned his attention to Samee, his hands reaching for her with the desperate hunger of someone seeking validation. But she, too, pulled away, her own emotional state too fragile for intimacy.

"I'm going to check on Valou."

The bathroom door stood slightly ajar, steam escaping into the hallway like ghostly fingers. Samee pushed it open to find Valouna standing under the rainfall showerhead, water cascading over her dark skin in silver rivulets. Her eyes were closed, face tilted upward as if seeking absolution from the heavens.

"Why can't you love me. I promise I can make you happy."

The words emerged raw and unfiltered, torn from some deep place where Valouna kept her most vulnerable truths. They hung in the steam-filled air like a prayer.

"You're not invisible to me, my luv. I do love you so much."

What happened next unfolded with the inevitability of gravity. Their lips met under the spray of hot water, hands exploring familiar territory with desperate urgency. The bathroom filled with the sounds of their passion—soft moans mixing with the percussion of water against tile.

John approached the bathroom to offer his apology, his footsteps muffled by the thick carpet. The door stood open just enough to reveal the scene within—Valouna on her knees, Samee's leg draped over her shoulder, both women lost in an intimate dance that excluded him entirely. A single tear traced down his cheek as he quietly closed the door, the salt mixing with the bitter taste of betrayal.

He gathered his jacket and wallet in silence, his movements mechanical as he processed what he'd witnessed. The irony wasn't lost on him—minutes earlier, both women had claimed exhaustion, yet here they were, consumed by passion he couldn't ignite. The Uber arrived as he stepped onto the sidewalk, the driver's casual greeting falling on deaf ears.

Ten minutes later, his phone buzzed with Samee's text: *"Come to the bedroom,"* followed by three heart emojis. But John's ego bore fresh wounds, and his pride wouldn't allow him to answer. He powered down the device and stared out the window as the city blurred past.

Back in the brownstone, Samee and Valou emerged from their aquatic sanctuary to find the living room empty. John's absence registered like a missing note in a familiar song. Samee felt the loss more acutely, her chest tightening with guilt and regret.

But Valouna saw an opportunity where Samee saw a crisis. This was her moment to demonstrate what life could offer if she were Samee's only lover, her singular focus. She held nothing back, pouring *every* ounce of skill and passion into their lovemaking as if competing with a ghost.

Thirty minutes into their encounter, Samee's face revealed the truth Valouna feared most—emotional distance disguised as physical pleasure. The recognition hit like a physical blow, but Valouna said nothing. She simply withdrew, arranging herself on the far side of the bed with her back turned.

Samee lay awake in the darkness, John's absence a palpable presence beside her. Her final text of the night—*"Goodnight, my love, missing you"* with three heart emojis—went unanswered. Beside her, Valouna's shoulders shook with silent tears, her pretense of sleep fooling no one.

The next morning arrived with the weight of unspoken apologies and unresolved tensions. John appeared at Valouna's door dressed as if he were auditioning for a spy thriller—his suit tailored to perfection, his jaw clean-shaven, his entire appearance exuding an air of expensive taste and meticulous attention to detail. The sight of him took Samee's breath away, reminding her why she'd fallen for him in the first place.

She wanted to address the previous night's events, to explain and apologize, and somehow bridge the chasm that had opened between them. But Laura's charity event loomed, and time was their enemy. The words remained trapped in her throat as they settled into John's luxury sedan, the leather seats creaking under their combined weight.

Valouna claimed the backseat, her hopes carefully hidden behind designer sunglasses. Perhaps tonight would be different. Maybe tonight, John and Samee would finally acknowledge her place in their unconventional family structure. The possibility hummed through her veins like electricity.

The venue sparkled with old money and new wealth, crystal chandeliers casting rainbow patterns across marble floors while waiters in crisp uniforms circulated with champagne flutes. The city's elite had gathered in their finest armor—women draped in silk and diamonds, men sharp in tailored suits, everyone performing their prescribed roles in the theater of high society.

Valouna and Samee emerged from the car hand in hand, their fingers intertwined with natural ease. But the moment Laura approached— John's sister, radiant in emerald silk— Samee's hand slipped away like smoke. Her fingers found John's instead, claiming him with territorial precision that left Valouna standing alone.

The rejection stung, but Valouna forced her features into a mask of pleasant indifference. This was neither the time nor the place for emotional displays. She fell into step behind them, playing her assigned role as the dutiful best friend while her heart cracked with each step.

The crowd parted before John and Samee like the Red Sea, their coupled presence drawing approving nods and whispered comments. They were the picture of perfection— successful, attractive, and socially connected—the ideal couple presenting their perfect life to an audience that valued appearances above authenticity.

"Remember to keep smiling. We need to maintain appearances," Samee whispered, her breath warm against

John's ear.

"It's all part of the act, isn't it?" John's response carried an edge that only she could detect.

Meanwhile, Valouna navigated the social currents with practiced grace, her smile never wavering even as each introduction drove the knife deeper. "This is Samee's best friend, Valouna." The words became a mantra, defining her place in their world with surgical precision.

Laura, ever the hostess, noticed Valouna's solitary state and misinterpreted it entirely. In her mind, Valouna's longing glances toward John and Samee spoke of romantic envy rather than romantic exclusion. The misunderstanding would prove catastrophic.

"Valouna, you don't have to look at your best friend with envy. I have one of the most handsome and very much single cousins, who's in your age bracket, named Kevin, and I think you two can really hit it off together."

The suggestion landed like a physical blow, but Laura's enthusiasm brooked no argument. Before Valouna could protest, she found herself face-to-face with Kevin—tall, conventionally handsome, and clearly smitten at first sight. His smile was warm and genuine, his interest obvious and flattering under different circumstances.

Across the room, another figure made her entrance with the dramatic flair of someone accustomed to commanding attention. Jennifer, John's ex-wife, swept through the crowd on the arm of her companion, Tom, her eyes scanning the room with predatory interest. She spotted Valouna first, still engaged in polite conversation with Kevin, and her brain made the natural assumption.

So, this was Samee, John's new girlfriend. But wait—who was that other woman hanging on John's arm?

"Look, there's John...with another woman!" she whispered to Tom, her voice sharp with confusion and something that might have been jealousy.

"Are you sure that's what you think, Jen?" Tom's response carried the weary tone of someone accustomed to managing his companion's dramatic tendencies.

"That woman, Samee—I thought she was John's girlfriend. Who's this new woman with him?"

The misunderstanding spread like a virus, multiplying confusion in Jennifer's mind as she tried to piece together a puzzle with deliberately scattered pieces. Her eyes darted between Valouna and Samee, trying to decode the relationships she was witnessing.

Valouna excused herself from Kevin with diplomatic grace, her instincts warning her of approaching danger. She moved toward John and Samee with practiced casualness, but her message was urgent: Jennifer was here, and their careful charade was about to be tested.

The three of them huddled in a heated discussion, their voices low but their body language screaming tension. Samee was reluctant to continue their deception, but John seemed lost in his own emotional fog, indifferent to the approaching storm.

When Jennifer finally approached, her smile as sharp as a blade, Valouna made her choice. Her arm slipped through John's with possessive confidence as she transformed herself into Samee, the girlfriend, the chosen one. Samee stepped back reluctantly, playing along with a performance that left her feeling hollowed out and discarded.

"Sometimes it feels like I'm just a spectator, even when we're together," John confessed to Samee during a brief moment of privacy, his voice heavy with exhaustion.

"You mean everything to me, John. Please don't start this right now."

The game continued, with each of them playing multiple roles as the evening demanded. Around Laura and her friends, John and Samee performed as the happy couple. Around Jennifer, John, and Valouna pretended to be the established pair. The mental gymnastics required to maintain their various personas left them all drained.

Jennifer watched from the sidelines with growing suspicion, her trained eye catching the subtle inconsistencies in their performance.

Something was definitely wrong with this picture, but she couldn't quite identify the missing piece.

The pressure became unbearable. Valouna slipped away to find solitude, her composed facade finally cracking under the strain. The bathroom became her sanctuary, its marble surfaces and soft lighting providing temporary refuge from the performance outside.

"Valou, please try to understand. I care deeply for you," Samee followed her, her voice carrying genuine anguish.

"I can't keep hiding us, Samee. It's breaking me apart." The words tore from Valouna's throat, raw and desperate.

Outside, Jennifer continued her surveillance, her suspicions crystallizing into certainty. "That woman looks upset. Something's definitely going on."

The final act began when Jennifer approached Kevin, her curiosity overriding social etiquette. A few carefully phrased questions revealed the truth she'd been seeking: the woman who had introduced herself as Samaya was actually named Valouna.

Armed with this revelation, Jennifer approached John with the righteous fury of someone who believed she was exposing infidelity. The irony of his ex-wife defending his current girlfriend's honor was lost on everyone in that moment.

"So, this is how you treat Samee? Who is this woman, and why is she here with you?"

The confrontation erupted with volcanic force, drawing the attention of everyone in the ballroom. Voices rose, accusations flew, and their carefully constructed facade crumbled like a house of cards in a hurricane.

Valouna had reached her breaking point. The months of hiding, pretending, and being invisible while desperately wanting to be seen—all culminated in this moment of brutal honesty.

"I don't know if I've been in a relationship with Samee and John, but I've definitely been sleeping with them sometimes. but I can't do this anymore, I'm tired of being invisible."

The words detonated like a bomb, silencing the room with their shocking revelation. Laura's face went white. Jennifer's mouth fell open. Even the waitstaff paused in their duties, sensing the dramatic shift in the evening's energy.

Kevin approached Valouna with wounded dignity, his earlier interest curdling into disgust. "I don't think I want to have dinner with you anymore."

Valouna's smile held no warmth, only bitter satisfaction. "Don't worry yourself, I don't want to have anything to do with anyone in your family ever again."

She walked toward the exit with her head high, her dignity intact despite the carnage she was leaving behind. John exhaled slowly. For a second, he couldn't look at her. Everything felt loud in the room, the people, the weight of every decision they had made pressing in on him from all sides. He had thought he could handle it, thought he could keep up, thought he could be enough for both of them. But standing there now, he felt tired. Not physically-something deeper. Like he had been trying to hold together something that was never meant to stay whole, and he no longer had the strength to keep pretending.

John watched her go with something that might have been admiration, then turned to Samee with exhaustion etched into every line of his face.

"Samee, this is too much for me. I'm an old man; in seven more years, I'll be fifty. I'm sorry, I can't be with you anymore."

His departure left Samee standing alone in the wreckage of their relationship, surrounded by curious faces and whispered speculation. The tears came finally, hot and bitter as they traced down her cheeks. The perfect life they'd performed for so many months had imploded spectacularly, leaving nothing but debris and regret.

The weeks that followed stretched like a wound that refused to heal. John sat in his apartment, the leather couch creaking under his restless movement as he stared at the television without seeing. A beer bottle sweated in his palm, the label peeling under his absent-minded picking. The latenight talk show host's voice blended into the background noise, filling the silence with meaningless chatter that offered no comfort.

His apartment felt cavernous, every corner echoing with memories he couldn't escape. The image of Valouna walking away, of Samee's tears, of his own cowardly retreat—they played on a constant loop in his mind like a broken film reel.

"What the hell am I doing..." The words emerged as barely a whisper, swallowed by the empty room.

His phone sat on the coffee table like an accusation, its dark screen reflecting his haggard face. His finger hovered over it repeatedly, muscle memory pulling him toward connection, but courage failing him each time. What could he possibly say to either of them? How could he explain choices he didn't understand himself?

Across town, Valouna thrashed in sheets that smelled only of her own loneliness. The king-sized bed felt infinite, its empty expanse mocking her solitude. Moonlight filtered through gauze curtains, casting everything in silver and shadow.

Sleep eluded her, chased away by the phantom warmth of bodies that were no longer there. She sat up finally, pulling the silk comforter around her shoulders like armor against the night. Her phone glowed with notifications—messages from John, from Samee, digital olive branches she couldn't bring herself to accept.

The window drew her like a magnet, the city spreading below in patterns of light and darkness. Somewhere out there, John was drinking alone. Somewhere, Samee was crying. The knowledge sat heavily in her chest, but pride held her paralyzed.

"I miss them." The admission escaped like a prayer, but the empty room offered no absolution.

Samee's bedroom resembled a war zone—clothes scattered like casualties, her laptop abandoned on the floor, the detritus of a life falling apart. She lay amid the chaos, staring at water stains on the ceiling that resembled maps to nowhere.

Her phone buzzed against the nightstand, and hope leaped in her chest before crashing down again. Janelle's name glowed on the screen, her message no doubt full of gossip and false sympathy. The woman had an uncanny ability to appear whenever drama struck, like a vulture circling fresh roadkill.

"Why do I miss them so much?" The question hung in the air, unanswered and unanswerable.

Two weeks crawled by with the sluggish pace of healing wounds. Life, indifferent to personal tragedy, continued its relentless march forward. Samee stood in her agent's office, signing contracts for a new modeling campaign with mechanical precision. When asked if she knew any additional models for the shoot, she could recommend. She slipped on her designer sunglasses, as if they were a mask. "No, I don't."

The lie came easily, self-preservation overriding loyalty. The world she'd shared with Valouna had ended, and there was no going back.

John found himself pushed toward normalcy by well-meaning family members. His brother-in-law orchestrated a date with Margarette, a woman whose conversation revolved around marriage prospects with the single-minded focus of a heat-seeking missile. No matter how desperately John tried to redirect their discussions, she found ways to circle back to wedding plans and shared futures.

The contrast was stark and depressing. Where Samee and Valou had challenged him, excited him, and made him feel young again, Margarette offered only safe predictability.

Perhaps that was exactly what he needed—the kind of woman who wouldn't turn his world upside down, who wouldn't make him question everything he thought he understood about love and desire.

The following week, John made a decision that surprised even himself. He purchased a private plane, making a substantial down payment and arranging financing for the rest. The Cessna Citation sat gleaming on the tarmac like a promise of freedom, the first tangible step toward his dream of starting JSV Airlines LLC.

Standing beside the aircraft, he could almost see them— Samee and Valouna in matching bikinis, jumping up and down with infectious enthusiasm, celebrating his courage to bet on himself. The phantom image was so vivid he could hear their laughter carried on the wind.

But when he blinked, he stood alone on the empty tarmac, the silence broken only by the distant hum of jet engines and the hollow sound of his own breathing. The plane represented more than a business investment—it was a declaration of independence, a symbol of the life he was building from the ashes of the one that had imploded.

The future stretched before him, uncertain but undeniably his own. Whether Samee and Valouna would be part of that future remained to be seen, but for now, John was learning to fly solo, one decision at a time.

CHAPTER 10
FACING TRUTH

The silence in Samaya's condo pressed against her eardrums like deep water, each tick of the antique clock on her mantle marking time with surgical precision. She sat curled into the corner of her Italian leather sectional, her phone clutched in both hands as if it were a lifeline connecting her to a world she'd lost. The device's weight seemed disproportionate to its size—heavy with the gravity of decisions unmade, words unspoken, relationships hanging in digital limbo.

The living room around her reflected the careful curation of someone who understood that appearances mattered. Floor-to-ceiling windows offered a panoramic view of the city's glittering sprawl, but tonight the lights blurred together like teardrops on glass. Abstract art hung on exposed brick walls—expensive pieces chosen more for their investment potential than emotional resonance. Everything spoke of success, sophistication, control—everything except the woman drowning in the center of it all.

Her thumb traced circles across the phone's surface, leaving ghostly smudges on the pristine screen. The contact list glowed with names that had once meant everything— before the charity event, before the revelations, before their carefully constructed world had imploded spectacularly. Two names commanded her attention with magnetic force: John and Valouna. The architects of her happiness and the engineers of her destruction, bound together in her phone's memory like former lovers sharing the same bed.

The apartment's climate control hummed with mechanical efficiency, but Samaya's skin prickled with nervous energy that no temperature adjustment could remedy. Her breath came in shallow sips, each inhalation carrying the lingering scent of her expensive perfume mixed with something sharper—the metallic taste of fear coating her tongue.

A decision crystallized like ice forming on a winter glass. Her thumb moved with deliberate precision, selecting John's name from the digital gallery of her past. The phone rang once, twice, each tone reverberating through her chest cavity like church bells announcing the end of something sacred.

"Samaya? What's up?"

His voice carried across the connection with cautious warmth, the familiar baritone that had once whispered promises against her skin now filtered through electromagnetic waves and careful distance. She could picture him wherever he was—probably his apartment, maybe pacing the hardwood floors she'd walked barefoot across so many mornings, running his free hand through graying hair that she'd once threaded her fingers through.

"John... we need to talk. I want you to come over. Tonight."

The words emerged with more confidence than she possessed, each syllable measured and delivered with the precision of someone who understood that retreat was no longer an option. The silence that followed stretched like a tightrope, fraught with the weight of everything they'd said and everything they hadn't.

"Are you sure? After everything?"

His question carried layers—hurt, hope, hesitation wound together like DNA strands forming something complex and fragile. She could hear the television murmuring in the background, some late-night program providing a soundtrack to his solitude. The normalcy of it struck her as both comforting and heartbreaking.

"Yeah. We can't keep avoiding this."

Truth rang in her voice like a bell struck true. The weeks of silence had solved nothing, healed nothing, resolved nothing. They'd simply allowed the wounds to fester in darkness, growing more infected with each passing day of deliberate avoidance.

John's exhale crackled through the speaker, a sound weighted with resignation and something that might have been relief. Behind his careful hesitation, she could sense the truth he'd been hiding from himself—he loved her. The pretending, the distance, the wounded pride—it was all theater performed for an audience of one—his own stubborn heart.

John didn't answer right away. For a moment, he just stood there with the phone pressed to his ear, staring at nothing. He could already feel it-the pull, the same pull that had brought him back every time, no matter how much he tried to convince himself he was done. Part of him wanted to say no, to stay exactly where he was, to protect whatever was left of him. But another part, the part he couldn't silence was already on his way."Alright. I'll be there."

"Good, see you tonight."

The line went dead with surgical finality, leaving Samaya staring at the phone's screen as if it might offer some clue about what was to come next. Her reflection stared back from the black surface—hollow-eyed, angular with stress, beautiful in the way that broken things sometimes achieved unexpected grace.

Her hands trembled with barely controlled energy as she navigated back to her contacts. Valouna's name appeared like a prayer written in pixels, each letter carrying the weight of conversations they'd never had, truths they'd never spoken, a love that had no name in any language she understood.

The phone rang with the same mechanical precision, but this call felt different—more dangerous, more necessary, more likely to destroy whatever fragile equilibrium she'd managed to maintain since that disastrous night at the charity event.

"Hey."

Valouna's voice came through the speaker like smoke— soft, cautious, carrying undertones of hurt that three weeks hadn't managed to diminish. The single word contained multitudes: anger, longing, resignation, hope, all compressed into three letters, one word that somehow encompassed their entire complicated history.

"Valouna... I need to see you. Can you come over tonight? We need to talk."

The confession spilled out in a rush, propelled by momentum she couldn't control. Her heart hammered against her ribs like a caged bird, each beat echoing in her ears with deafening intensity. The city lights beyond her windows blurred and sharpened in rhythm with her pulse, as if the entire world was keeping time with her anxiety.

Silence stretched across the connection like a bridge neither of them was certain they wanted to cross. She could picture Valouna in her renovated brownstone, probably sitting in that impossibly comfortable reading chair by the window, wrapped in silk pajamas that cost more than most people's monthly rent, beautiful even in solitude.

"Is John going to be there?"

The question arrived sharp as a blade, cutting straight to the heart of their triangle. Valouna's voice carried no judgment, only weary acceptance of a reality none of them had chosen but all of them had helped create. She understood, without explanation, that this wasn't about choosing sides or exclusion. This was about facing the music they'd all been dancing to.

Samaya's eyes closed involuntarily; lids heavy with the weight of honesty. "Yeah, he is. I want us to talk... all of us. It's time."

The words hung in the air like incense, carrying prayers and confessions to whatever Gods governed matters of the heart. She could hear Valouna breathing on the other end, the soft rhythm of someone calculating costs and benefits with the precision of an accountant auditing her own soul.

"Alright. I'll come."

Valou's sigh crackled through the speaker—a sound like wind through autumn leaves, carrying resignation and courage in equal measure. The line went dead, leaving Samaya alone with the consequences of her decisions and the weight of anticipation pressing against her chest like a physical presence.

She lowered the phone to her lap and stared into the middle distance, her gaze both unfocused and intense at the same time. The apartment around her seemed to hold its breath, as if the walls themselves understood the significance of what was about to unfold within their embrace.

"This is it."

The words escaped her lips unbidden, a whispered acknowledgment that she'd set something in motion that couldn't be stopped, undone, or redirected. Like a stone thrown into still water, the ripples would spread outward until they touched every corner of their shared lives.

She leaned back into the leather cushions, her body sinking into expensive comfort that felt more like quicksand. Her mind raced through possibilities, scenarios, potential outcomes—each one more complex and uncertain than the last. What would she say when they arrived? How could she explain the inexplicable? How could she make them understand what she barely understood herself?

The clock on the mantle continued its relentless countdown, each tick a small death, each tock a small birth. Time moved forward with mechanical indifference, carrying her toward a confrontation that would either heal their fractured triangle or shatter it beyond repair.

Her reflection caught her eye in the black television screen across the room—a ghost image of herself superimposed over the dark surface like a photograph double-exposed with emptiness. She appeared fragile and fierce simultaneously, vulnerable yet determined, beautiful in the way that desperate things sometimes achieved unexpected power.

The city beyond her windows pulsed with its eternal rhythm—millions of lives intersecting and diverging in patterns too complex for any single mind to comprehend. Somewhere in that vast urban maze, John was gathering his keys, checking his appearance in bathroom mirrors, preparing himself for a conversation that might change everything. Somewhere else, Valouna was choosing her armor—probably something elegant and understated that would make her look effortlessly stunning while secretly providing emotional protection.

And here she sat, the axis around which their complicated dance revolved, the eye of a storm she'd helped create through equal measures of love and cowardice, desire and fear, honesty and deception.

The apartment's silence grew thicker, more oppressive, pregnant with possibility and dread. She could feel the weight of impending arrival—two separate journeys converging on her living room like freight trains approaching the same intersection. The impact was inevitable now, the timing beyond her control.

Her phone lay silent in her lap, its purpose served, its digital magic exhausted. The device that had once connected them now seemed as obsolete as smoke signals, insufficient for the complex emotional mathematics they were about to attempt. What came next would require presence, proximity, the messy intimacy of breathing the same air and occupying the same space.

Minutes crawled by with geological slowness, each one adding another layer to her anxiety like sediment accumulating on an ocean floor. She found herself cataloging the details of her surroundings with obsessive precision—the way shadows fell across the hardwood floors, the distant hum of traffic filtering through the expensive windows, and the subtle scent of vanilla candles mixing with the leather and lemon oil that permeated her carefully curated space.

These might be the last moments of peace she'd experience for a very long time. Soon, her sanctuary would be invaded by the complicated geometry of their relationship, transforming it from a refuge into a battlefield. The leather sectional where she'd spent countless evenings alone would become a stage for the most important performance of her life.

Her breathing slowed as she settled into the waiting, her nervous system finding some measure of equilibrium in the face of impending chaos. Whatever happened next, whatever words were spoken or left unspoken, whatever decisions were made or avoided—she would face it with the dignity befitting someone who had finally stopped running from her own heart.

The city lights continued their eternal dance beyond her windows, indifferent to human drama yet somehow reassuring in their constancy. Life would continue regardless of whether their triangle survived or disintegrated. The world would keep turning, hearts would keep beating, the sun would rise tomorrow on whatever landscape emerged from tonight's reckoning.

But for now, in the fragile bubble of her living room, suspended between past and future like an insect preserved in amber, Samaya waited. She waited for the sound of elevators ascending, for footsteps in hallways, for the soft chime of her doorbell announcing that the time for waiting was over.

The silence stretched on, no longer oppressive but almost peaceful—the calm before a storm that would either wash them clean or drown them completely. Either way, she would no longer be alone with her secrets, her fears, her impossible love for two people who had become essential as breathing and dangerous as gravity.

The reckoning was coming, and she was ready to face whatever truths emerged from the collision of their separate worlds. The time for pretending was over. The time for truth had finally begun.

ACT III:
The Resolution

CHAPTER 11
THE SUMMONS

Valouna leaned back against the wall, her heart heavy with thoughts she couldn't shake. The night air buzzed outside her window, but inside her chest, it was still and tense. How had she let Samee place her back in the same position again? Three weeks of loneliness made her think back to the last time she tried to dream of a life with Samee. Those memories, she never ordered, but they came with the platter of chaos that nearly swallowed her whole?

Samee was always the smooth talker, the one who could smile her way through a storm and make hell look like a holiday. Back then, it was this bad boy named Nine8 Kill, Samee's fast-talking self, drug-dealing, swagger-heavy boyfriend who had dreams of power and two women on his arm like trophies.

Valouna had hesitated. Her heart wasn't in it, not for him. It had always been Samee that stirred something real in her. But Samee had insisted. "Let's just try it for one night," she'd whispered. "He's rough, but he's got a good side too."

Against her better judgment, Valouna agreed. One night couldn't hurt, right?

That night started with them rolling up to Roscoe's Chicken & Things just after 1 AM. It was a hole-in-the-wall kind of place, but the smell of fried chicken and collard greens could bring peace to even the roughest souls. The crowd was mostly post-party folks, sprinkled with local gangsters, hustlers, and shady night owls who did more talking with their eyes than their mouths.

They sat in a red leather booth, under flickering lights, sharing plates of greasy food while Nine8 bragged about a "business opportunity" he had coming up. Valouna watched him closely. He was all gold chains, slick words, and aggressive charm. She could feel the tension in his body even when he smiled, like a coiled snake waiting to strike.

That's when it happened. A guy from another table walked by, bold as ever, and gave Samee a full-body look before letting out a soft whistle.

Nine8 stood up instantly. "Who the hell you looking' at, clown?" he snapped.

The man smirked. "Just admiring the scenery, bro."

The next thing Valouna knew, punches were flying. Chairs flipped. Glass broke. Nine8 slammed the guy against the wall, shouting, "Those two women are my bitches, stupid ass motherfucker! You need to learn how to respect another man's women."

The place exploded into chaos. Security rushed in, but no one stopped Nine8. When it was over, the guy was bleeding on the floor, and Nine8 walked back like a king who had just defended his throne.

Valouna sat frozen, trying to hide the fear rushing through her. Samee, ever calm, wiped her mouth with a napkin like nothing had happened. "He's protective," she said, like that explained it all.

Valouna wanted to run then, but she didn't. Samee was the only one who made her heart beat with love drums. So, she stayed.

They left Roscoe's under the buzz of flickering neon and sirens in the distance. Samee wrapped her arm around Valouna's waist like nothing had happened, like they were just three friends heading home from a regular night out.

But Valouna's mind was racing.

Samee whispered in her ear, "Don't judge him too fast. Nine8's been through a lot. He just needs someone to believe in him."

Valouna gave a tight nod, her jaw clenched. It wasn't Nine8 she believed in. It was Samee. Always Samee.

Five days passed, and after a night of clubbing, they ended up at Nine8's condo in Spanish Harlem. His apartment was filled with smoke, neon lighting, and the faint smell of weed and cologne. Loud trap music vibrated from the walls, but even louder was the tension between the three of them. Valouna knew she should have left. Every instinct screamed it. But she was trying her best to see Nine8 like Samee sees him.

Samee touched her shoulder gently, "Stay the night, just this once."

Valouna didn't say yes. She didn't say no either.

That night, something wild happened. Maybe it was the music, the leftover adrenaline from the fight almost a week ago, or the way Samee looked at her with those eyes like secrets. But Valou gave in. The three of them tangled in a passion that felt more like war than love. Every touch was intense, every kiss like a dare. Nine8 tried to dominate, to impress, but Valouna's eyes kept finding Samee's.

And Samee... Samee made it all feel dangerous and beautiful at the same time.

Afterward, Nine8 lit a blunt and said, "I got something for y'all. Something big."

He talked about ZoGod's modeling event, hyping it like a golden ticket. "You two? You're stars. I'm gonna get you in. I know people."

What he didn't say was that the event was a front. ZoGod ran a whole empire under the table, guns, pills, fake glamor. The runway was just a cover for deals that ended in violence. Valouna and Samee stepped into that world wearing heels and confidence, but they didn't know they were walking into a trap.

That night, at the event, things spiraled out of control quickly.

ZoGod couldn't believe his eyes. A low hanging fruit like Nine8, walking inside his party, word to his mama with two actual baddies. He waited until he went out to get some drinks and he creek-up from behind and made a pass at Samee and Valou in front of everyone. Called them "Rare breed." Offered them the world if they left Nine8. Nine8 saw it and played it cool. Samee and Valou respectfully turned down ZoGod's advance. "Ya bitches must be pure lesbians; I'm trying to level you two bitches up. Respectfully, Nine8 is an ugly motherfucker compared to me, and ya, turned me down? Really." ZoGod looked flabbergasted.

Then came the smooth-talking stranger, a man who looked too clean, too sharp. Trying to make them believe, he's the other famous SnowMan. And if they role with him, they would never experience the word need cause whatever their hearts' desire... it's already All There. The gift and the curse of being a beautiful woman, you always have to master the skill to politely stop unwanted advances. Seeing they didn't fall for his games, later that night, behind the curtains, he confessed to both girls in a whisper: "I'm with the FBI. My real name is Gil Arenas. I'm here to bring ZoGod down. But... damn... y'all got me Keith Sweating twisted. I ain't never seen beauty like you two in my life. Tell me what I have to do for you two to be mine."

Agent Gil wasn't playing undercover anymore. He was caught in it, just like they were.

ZoGod overheard. His eyes went cold. And that was the beginning of the end.

ZoGod's face shifted the second he heard Agent Arenas' confession. His laid-back swagger dropped, and the room suddenly felt colder. His gold chains glinted under the spotlight, but his eyes were all shadows.

His mind had one singular thought: "How to kill this FBI agent and get away with it? But first he gotta pee."

Nine8 saw ZoGod going into the bathroom and followed him, holding his gun tight underneath his jacket. His plan was to shoot that disrespectful motherfucker in the face, for trying to diss him and trying to bust down his ladies. Agent Gil Arenas followed right behind him, sensing something was about to go down. Agent Gil had no choice but to pull out his gun and save the life of the man he was trying to put behind bars for the rest of his life. Agent Gil Arenas took Nine8's life with just one bullet. And the dance between Agent Gil and ZoGod began that very day. Some even rumored, their story continued in Agent 009. Langichatte LaBond, you will get more insights between those two.

Back to Present Times

The glass doors whispered open as John stepped into the building's lobby, their movement so smooth it felt like entering another dimension. His footsteps echoed sharply against the polished Carrara marble, each tap of his leather soles amplified by the cathedral-like space above. The lobby stretched before him—all gleaming surfaces and muted lighting designed to intimidate and impress—but his attention snapped to the figure near the elevator bank like iron filings drawn to a magnet.

VALOUNA!

The name hit him with physical force, a punch to the solar plexus that left him momentarily breathless. She stood with her back to him, but he would have recognized that silhouette anywhere—the elegant line of her neck, the way she held her left shoulder slightly higher than her right, the particular grace with which she occupied space even when she thought no one was watching.

Three weeks. Three weeks since he'd seen her face, heard her voice, caught her scent in a crowded room. Twenty-one days had crawled by with the sluggish pace of wounded animals, each one marked by her absence like a physical ache. The separation had carved hollow spaces in his chest, spaces he'd tried to fill with sixteen-hour workdays, with silence, business improvements, with bourbon, with anything except the admission of what those spaces meant.

He had told himself the distance was necessary and healthy. The situation with Samee and Valou had become impossible to navigate. Truth be told, he felt like the third wheel in the relationship and at his sister Laura's event everything came to light. The decision to step away from both of them had seemed rational like getting up and go to work on a Monday morning. Yet, his heart is utterly fucking miserable, wishing he was back in the maze.

But seeing Valouna now, the careful architecture of his resolve began to crumble. She wore a charcoal wool coat that skimmed her knees, her dark hair twisted into a low chignon that exposed the vulnerable curve of her nape. Everything about her posture suggested wariness, as if she were braced for impact.

She turned, perhaps sensing his presence the way people sometimes do when they're being watched. Their eyes met across the expanse of marble and chrome, and the world seemed to contract to just that point of connection—two people recognizing something in each other that they'd both been trying to forget.

John's collar suddenly felt too tight, the silk tie he'd chosen that morning now seeming like a noose around his throat. He tugged at it, the fabric rough against his fingers as he approached, each step feeling both inevitable and terrifying. Valouna's hand found the strap of her leather bag—a cognaccolored vintage piece she'd seen at a flea market in Brooklyn— fidgeting with the worn material in a gesture he recognized as intimately as his own heartbeat. Her throat tightened when anxiety crept up her spine like spider legs.

The lobby's ambient music—some soulless elevator jazz— seemed to grow louder as the distance between them shrank. Neither had expected this collision, this cosmic joke of timing that had brought them to the same place at the same moment when they'd both been so carefully avoiding exactly this scenario. Neither had prepared for the way the air seemed to thicken between them, charged with unspoken words and unfinished conversations and the weight of everything they'd shared before it all went sideways.

"Hey." The word scraped out of his throat, awkward and insufficient, carrying none of the casual confidence he'd hoped for. It sounded like what it was—the greeting of a man who had spent three weeks rehearsing this moment and still had no idea what to say.

Valouna's nod was barely perceptible, a micro-movement that suggested she was fighting her own internal war between approach and retreat. Her gaze flickered toward the elevator as if the polished steel doors might offer escape from whatever this moment was becoming, from whatever Samee had orchestrated by summoning them both here. A soft breath escaped her lips—resignation, perhaps, or the exhale before diving into deep water without knowing what lurked beneath the surface.

They walked toward the elevator in silence, their footsteps creating a mismatched rhythm on the marble—his heavier, more decisive, hers lighter but somehow more deliberate. The building's other occupants seemed to fade into background noise, their conversations and phone calls becoming meaningless static against the electric tension that crackled between John and Valouna like a live wire.

The silver doors parted with a quiet hiss, revealing the cramped interior that would hold them captive for twenty-six floors. The elevator was one of those expensive, minimalist affairs—brushed steel walls, a single row of buttons, no mirrors to complicate an already complicated situation. John could smell the faint scent of industrial cleaning products mixed with something else—the accumulated weight of a thousand awkward conversations that had taken place in this vertical prison.

John's finger stabbed the button for the twenty-sixth floor with more force than necessary, the small act of aggression providing momentary relief from the tension coiling in his chest. The elevator lurched upward with mechanical precision, and the soft hum of the motor filled the space between them like a third presence, unwelcome and persistent. The digital display above the doors began its steady climb: 12, 13, 14.

The silence stretched, heavy and elastic, threatening to snap under its own weight. John pressed his spine against the cool metal wall, the chill seeping through his wool suit jacket and into his skin. His hands buried themselves deep in his pockets, where his fingers could clench and unclench without betraying the anxiety that was eating him alive from the inside out.

He stood an arm's length away—close enough to catch the faint vanilla of her perfume mixed with something earthier, something that was purely her, far enough to maintain the pretense of indifference they were both desperately trying to perform. She had lost weight, he realized with a sharp pang of concern. Her cheekbones were more pronounced, her collarbones more visible above the neckline of her dress. The separation had been hard on her as well.

The space was too small, the air too thin, the forced proximity a cruel joke played by whoever designed buildings to require vertical transportation. The three weeks of separation had been pure torture, each day stretching like a year, each night filled with dreams of her laugh, her touch, her presence in his bed. The hunger to bridge the gap between them gnawed at his ribs like a living thing, demanding acknowledgment, demanding action, demanding that he close the distance and damn the consequences.

But he couldn't. Not yet.

The floor numbers blinked past with maddening slowness. Fifteen. Sixteen. Seventeen. Each digit brought them closer to whatever confrontation awaited, each floor a countdown to a conversation that could either heal what had been broken or shatter it beyond repair.

Valouna shifted her weight from one foot to the other, a small movement that somehow conveyed volumes about her internal state. She studied the elevator's ceiling as if the acoustic tiles might hold answers to questions she was afraid to ask aloud. Her arms crossed over her chest, a barrier against the uncertainty that filled the small space like smoke, thick and choking and impossible to escape.

"I didn't expect..." She trailed off, her voice catching on something—regret, maybe, or the weight of words she'd been carrying for three weeks without anyone to share them with. Then she started again, her voice stronger, more determined: "Any of this."

The statement hung between them, encompassing everything—their meeting here, the complicated mess their relationship had become, the way loving two people had somehow made them strangers to both. John felt the truth of it settle in his chest like a stone dropped into still water, sending ripples through everything he thought he understood about desire and consequence.

John's eyes found hers in the reflection of the steel doors, then turned to meet them directly. The look that passed between them was raw, unguarded, stripped of the careful politeness they'd been maintaining since stepping into the elevator. "Neither did I."

In those three words lay acknowledgment of everything they'd lost, everything they'd hoped for, everything that had gone wrong since that first perfect night when the world had seemed full of infinite possibility. They had been walking blind ever since, stumbling through a landscape they didn't understand, making decisions without maps, guides, or any clear sense of where they were trying to go.

The look they shared lasted only seconds, but in that brief connection lay recognition—they were both casualties of something larger than themselves, both walking blind into whatever storm Samaya had summoned them to weather. Two people who had found each other and lost each other and now stood suspended between past and future, between what was and what might have been.

The elevator chimed with crystalline precision. Twenty-six.

The sound seemed to echo longer than it should have, hanging in the air like a bell tolling for something that had died without ceremony. The digital display glowed accusingly: 26. They had arrived at their destination, but neither moved toward the doors. For a moment, they existed in a state of suspended animation, caught between the safety of this small space and whatever lay beyond those steel barriers.

The doors slid open with mechanical indifference, revealing a carpeted hallway lined with abstract art and potted plants.

John and Valouna stepped out together, not quite touching but moving in unconscious synchrony, two people bracing themselves for impact. The elevator doors whispered shut behind them, cutting off their line of retreat, sealing their fate with the soft finality of expensive engineering.

Somewhere down the hall, behind a door marked with 2603 in tasteful silver numbers, in building three at Waterline Square, their future was waiting.

Their key fobs still grant them access. After three weeks of silence, of questions without answers, of sleeping alone in beds that felt too wide— those keyless key fobs were never removed out the system, that gave them entry to Samaya's condo. Yet John found himself pressing the doorbell anyway, Valouna beside him doing the same. As if the simple act of unlocking the door would presume too much, assume too much about where they stood.

The door clicked open. Samaya appeared in the narrow opening, her face a careful mask of composure that didn't quite conceal the tension in her jaw and the tightness around her eyes. She stepped back, ushering them inside with a gesture that was both welcoming and wary.

"I'm glad you both came." Her voice carried the forced calm of someone walking a tightrope. "You both already know the layout of this place, so please come have a seat."

She moved past them toward the living room, her bare feet silent on the hardwood. But instead of settling into one of the plush chairs or the sectional sofa, she continued toward the floor-to-ceiling windows that showcased the city's glittering skyline. Her back to them, she stood silhouetted against the lights, a figure carved from shadows and uncertainty.

John and Valouna exchanged glances—a wordless conversation of raised eyebrows and tightened mouths. The gravity of the moment pressed down on them like a physical weight, making even breathing feel deliberate.

"Samaya." John's voice cut through the silence, rough with unease. "What is this about? What's going on?"

She didn't turn. Didn't answer. Instead, she moved away from the window with deliberate steps, each footfall measured and purposeful. She walked past them without meeting their eyes, disappearing down the hallway that led to her bedroom.

The silence that followed was suffocating. John stood rooted near the island that separated the kitchen from the living room, his hands clenched at his sides. Valouna had moved toward the living room but stopped short of sitting, as if claiming a seat would somehow commit her to whatever was coming.

The sound of a door opening echoed down the hallway. Then closing. Then the footsteps returned.

"What the hell is happening?" Valouna's whisper was sharp with confusion and growing alarm.

Before John could formulate an answer, Samaya reappeared. But the woman who walked back into the living room was not the same one who had left. She was naked.

John's breath caught in his throat. His eyes widened, his mind struggling to process what he was seeing. Beside him, Valouna's lips parted, a small sound escaping—surprise, shock, something between a gasp and a sigh.

Samaya moved with purpose, unashamed of her nudity, her skin pale and luminous in the apartment's soft lighting. She settled onto the middle section of the sectional sofa, her legs parted slightly, her posture open and vulnerable yet somehow commanding.

Samaya opened her mouth, then stopped. For a second, nothing came out. Her hands trembled slightly against her thighs, her breath catching as if her body itself was trying to stop her from saying what she already knew would change everything. She looked at John, then at Valou, and for the first time since they walked in, she looked afraid. "I need to be honest with both of you." Her voice trembled slightly, but she pressed on, drawing a deep breath that made her ribcage expand and contract visibly. "I... I've been lying to both of you. To myself, really. I recognized the type of man John was from the beginning."

John's jaw tightened. He remained standing, his body rigid with tension, while Valouna slowly lowered herself onto the sofa portion to

Samaya's left. Seeing Valou sitting down, John claimed the loveseat to the right, creating a triangle of bodies and unspoken intentions.

"I realized he's exactly the type of man Valouna would fall in love with. I planned everything. I bought those Broadway tickets two days after I received the payment for the France gig."

Tears began to gather in Samaya's eyes, making them shine like glass in the lamplight. Her voice cracked as she continued, each word seeming to cost her something vital.

"I wanted you two to fall in love with each other. Not just with me. But the truth is..." She leaned forward, closing the distance between herself and her audience, tears now streaming freely down her cheeks.

"You what?" John's voice was barely audible, rough with confusion and something else—hurt, perhaps, or betrayal.

Samaya moved closer, her naked body trembling with the force of her emotions. "I love both of you equally. Valou, my love, I love eating your pussy, and I also love John's cock. I need you both in my life. I want... no, I need you two to love each other the same way I love you both. All I know is that life would be cruel if you force me to live without you both."

The words hung in the air like smoke, visible and choking. Valouna's face softened, her anger giving way to something more complex—understanding, perhaps, or recognition of the pain behind Samaya's confession.

"Samaya..." Valouna's voice was gentle now, stripped of its earlier edge.

"Valou, my love, I'm sorry I never acknowledged you in public. I wanted John to fall in love with you, too, before I did."

John finally spoke, his words careful and measured. "You say you love us both the same, yet you two seem more comfortable with each other than you do with me."

Samaya shook her head, her tears falling faster now. "There are going to be days when I only want Valou, or vice versa. Just like there'll be days when you only want to make love to Valou with her beautiful breasts. If you want the three of us to work, you're going to have to be okay with that."

Valouna leaned forward, her voice filled with both empathy and confusion. "If I wanted to have sex with John without you, you'd be absolutely okay with it?"

"Yes, yes... a million times yes." Samaya's entire body trembled with the force of her admission. "The thought of it turns me on. So I would have one request..."

"Which is?" Valouna's voice was barely a whisper.

"I would love to watch."

The confession settled over them like a blanket—heavy, warm, suffocating. John and Valouna exchanged another glance, this one longer, more searching. In it was the recognition of something they'd both been avoiding, something that had been building between them even as they'd orbited around Samaya's gravitational pull.

CHAPTER 12
CONVERGENCE

Samaya rose from the sofa, her naked form graceful despite the tremor in her limbs. She stood in the center of her living room like a supplicant, her breath coming in shallow gasps that made her ribcage flutter. The emotional weight of her confession had left her drained, hollow-eyed, and shaking.

She wiped the tears from her cheeks with the back of her hand, then drew a deep, shuddering breath that seemed to pull strength from some hidden reserve.

"I'm going to my bedroom now." Her voice was steadier than it had been, though still threaded with vulnerability. "If you both choose to come to my bedroom, I promise to love you both for the rest of my life. I promise never to embarrass us in public. I promise to tell you both, every day, how much I'm in love with you—both of you. Because I would never want either of you to think you're the third wheel. If you came into my room, I would make love to you both." In the morning, there would be consequences. Questions. Decisions that couldn't be unmade. Phone calls that would need to be made or avoided. Explanations that would either heal or destroy. The harsh light of day would force them to confront what they'd chosen in the forgiving darkness, to examine the beautiful mess they'd created and decide whether it was worth the cost.

But for now, Samee's only wish is for them to choose connection over caution, desire over safety, the beautiful complexity of hearts that refused to be confined by conventional boundaries.

As she closed her eyes, she saw them in her dream. Maybe, they all were dreaming at the same time. There was the weight of Valouna's body against his, the taste of Samee's skin, the sound of their breathing creating a rhythm that belonged to no one else in the world.

The lamp cast everything in a golden light, making them look like figures in a painting, something precious and rare, yet possibly doomed. John closed his eyes and let himself fall into the moment, into the space between intention and accident, between love and desire, between the people they'd been that morning and whoever they would become by dawn.

Outside, the city hummed its restless lullaby—sirens in the distance, the occasional rumble of late buses, the click of heels on sidewalks as other people lived other lives, made other choices. But inside this room, time moved differently, measured not in minutes but in heartbeats, in the soft sighs that escaped their lips, in the whispered words that would either bind them together or haunt them separately.

Samee shifted, her hair spilling across John's chest like dark water, and he felt the tremor that ran through her—not desire now, but something deeper. Fear, perhaps. Or the overwhelming weight of having gotten exactly what she'd wanted and not knowing if she was strong enough to hold onto it.

"Are you okay?" Valouna's voice was barely audible, her fingers tracing patterns on Samee's spine that could have been comfort or cartography, mapping the landscape of this new territory they'd entered together.

Samee nodded against John's chest, but her breathing was uneven, catching on something that might have been laughter or tears. "I keep thinking I'm going to wake up," she whispered. "That this is too good to be true."

John's hand found her hair, threading through the silk of it as he pressed a kiss to the crown of her head. "It's real," he said, and the certainty in his own voice surprised him. This man, who had spent years avoiding anything that couldn't be quantified or controlled, was suddenly anchored by something that defied all logic.

Valouna propped herself up on one elbow, studying their faces in the lamplight. There was something fierce in her expression, a determination that hadn't been there hours ago. "We're going to have to be brave," she said. "All of us. Braver than we've ever been."

The words hung in the air like a challenge, like a promise, like a prayer. They all knew what she meant. This wasn't just about tonight, about stolen hours in a room that smelled of jasmine and possibility. This was about choosing to rewrite the rules of their lives, to step outside the safe boundaries of what was expected and acceptable.

"My cousin DayDay is going to think I've lost my mind," Samee said with a shaky laugh. "She already thinks I make terrible decisions about men."

"Your cousin doesn't know us," John said softly. "She doesn't know this."

"No one knows this," Valouna added. "We're making it up as we go along."

There was something both terrifying and liberating about that admission. They were pioneers in uncharted territory, with no map, no guidebook, no precedent to follow. Just their hearts and their hope and the fierce conviction that what they'd found was worth fighting for.

The lamp flickered slightly, a brief reminder of the fragility of their golden cocoon. In a few hours, the sun would rise, and with it would come all the complications they were temporarily holding at bay. Work emails and family obligations, friends who would ask questions, and a society that would have opinions. The messy, demanding world that would insist on categorizing what couldn't be categorized, explaining what could only be felt.

But they also knew that some things were worth the cost. Some connections were rare enough to justify the risk. Some love was powerful enough to survive the harsh light of day, to weather the storms of judgment and doubt and uncertainty.

Samee lifted her head, looking between John and Valouna with eyes that were bright with unshed tears and something that might have been joy. "I want to try," she said. "I want to try to make this work, whatever it looks like, however impossible it seems."

"So do I," Valouna said immediately, her hand finding Samee's, then reaching for John's. "We'll figure out how to be us. We'll make our own rules."

John felt the weight of their trust, the magnitude of what they were asking of him and of each other. At his age, he'd thought he was done with grand gestures, with leaping into the unknown. But looking at these two extraordinary women who had somehow found their way into his carefully ordered life and turned it upside down, he knew he couldn't choose safety over possibility. Not this time.

"Yes," he said simply, squeezing their joined hands. "Yes, let's try."

The word seemed to release something in the room, a tension they hadn't even realized they'd been holding. They settled back into each other's arms, but the quality of their embrace had changed. It was no longer desperate or uncertain, but steady, grounded in decision and commitment.

They dozed intermittently as the night wore on, waking to touch and whisper and reassure each other that this was real, that they were choosing it, that tomorrow would bring its challenges but also its possibilities. They discussed practical matters—whose apartment was best suited for three people, how to navigate social situations, and when to tell their families—and more profound questions, such as whether love could truly conquer all, whether they were brave enough for this, and whether the world was ready for what they represented.

As the first pale light of dawn crept around the edges of the curtains, they made their final pact of the night. They would take it one day at a time. They would be patient with each other's fears and generous with each other's mistakes. They would remember that love, real love, was both simpler and more complicated than anyone ever expected.

And most importantly, they would trust what they'd found in the golden light of that lamp, in the space between who they'd been and who they were becoming, in the beautiful complexity of three hearts that had somehow learned to beat as one.

The morning would come, with all its consequences, questions, and harsh realities. But they would meet it together, and that made all the difference.

She paused as her eyes re-open… then moving between John and Valouna, memorizing their faces as if this might be the last time she saw them. "I saw us in my dreams. We can overcome everything. If neither of you shows up in my bedroom... understand that I will never love anyone the way I love you two. And I want to thank you both for the memories you shared with little old me."

Without another word, she turned and walked toward her bedroom, leaving the door ajar—an invitation as clear as it was unspoken. The soft sound of her sobs echoed faintly down the hallway as she disappeared into the dimly lit room.

John and Valouna remained in the living room, the silence between them thick as honey. They both stared at the open door, each lost in the maze of their own thoughts. The pull toward Samaya was undeniable— a magnetic force that seemed to tug at their very cores—but the complexity of what she was asking made processing it feel like swimming through concrete.

John exhaled slowly, running a hand through his hair. "I'm too old for all of this. I see now that sexy legs are the most demonic thing on earth."

His words lacked conviction, falling flat in the charged air between them. Deep down, they both recognized the truth in Samaya's confession—it wasn't irrational or desperate. It was raw, honest, and undeniably real.

Valouna released a slow breath, her heart hammering against her ribs like a caged bird. "I don't think you're old. I think you're mature." She paused, her voice dropping to barely above a whisper. "But do you think you could love me for the rest of your life?"

John's silence stretched between them like a bridge neither was sure they wanted to cross. The unspoken truth lingered in the air—they both felt something, not just for Samaya but for each other. It was a recognition that had been building for weeks, perhaps even months, hidden behind their shared devotion to the woman who had just bared her soul to them. Valouna stood, her body tense as if preparing for flight. She took a step toward the front door, her movement hesitant, uncertain. But before she could reach the exit, John moved.

"I do, I can love you for the rest of my life." His voice was quiet but firm, carrying a weight that made her stop mid-step.

She turned slowly, meeting his gaze. Something had shifted in his eyes—the walls he'd built around himself had cracked, revealing the vulnerability beneath. Without thinking, he closed the distance between them in three quick strides.

His hand found the back of her neck, fingers threading through her hair as he drew her face toward his. Their lips met in a kiss that was soft at first, tentative, questioning. But as Valouna melted against him, her arms winding around his waist, the kiss deepened, becoming urgent and desperate.

It wasn't just lust driving them—it was the emotion they'd been holding at bay, the love that had been growing in the shadows of their hearts. The kiss tasted of salt and possibility, of everything they'd been afraid to acknowledge.

When they finally broke apart, both breathing hard, they stood forehead to forehead for a moment, sharing the same air, the same space, the same understanding.

For a moment, neither of them moved. The silence between them wasn't empty; it was full-full of everything they hadn't said, full of everything they both understood now. John looked at her, not quickly, not by accident. He really looked. And in that moment, there was no confusion left, no pretending, no distance. Valouna felt it too the truth they had both been avoiding had finally caught up to them. This wasn't about Samaya anymore, not entirely. This was about them, and whether they were brave enough to stop running from it. Without words, they turned toward the hallway.

Their footsteps were silent on the hardwood floor, each step deliberate yet uncertain. The hallway stretched before them like a threshold between their old lives and whatever lay beyond. At Samaya's doorway, they paused, hands almost touching as they reached for the frame simultaneously.

Through the gap, they could see her silhouette against the window, moonlight painting silver streaks across her bare shoulders. She sat on the edge of the bed, her head bowed, fingers twisted together in her lap. The vulnerability in her posture made something deep in both their chests constrict.

John pushed the door open wider, the soft creak announcing their presence. Samaya's head lifted slowly, hope and fear warring in her expression as she saw them both standing

"You came," she whispered, and the relief in her voice was so profound it made Valouna's eyes well with tears.

"We're here," Valouna said softly, stepping into the room first. The space felt sacred somehow, charged with the weight of what they were choosing together.

John followed, closing the door gently behind them. "I've spent so many years being afraid," he said, his voice rough with emotion. "Afraid of being too much, or not enough. Afraid of wanting things I thought I had no right to want."

Samaya rose from the bed, taking a tentative step toward them. "And now?"

"Now I'm more afraid of walking away from this," he admitted. "From you. From both of you."

The three of them stood in a loose triangle, the air between them electric with possibility and uncertainty. It was Valouna who moved first, reaching out to take Samaya's hand, then John's, creating an unbroken circle.

"I've never done anything like this, actually giving my heart to two people." Valouna confessed, her voice barely audible. "I don't know the rules or how it's supposed to work."

"There are no rules," Samaya said, squeezing their hands. "Just us. Just this moment. Just choosing each other, however imperfectly."

John lifted their joined hands, pressing a kiss to Samaya's knuckles, then Valouna's. "Then we figure it out together. All of it. The good parts and the messy parts and everything in between."

The words hung in the air like a vow, binding them together in ways that went far deeper than physical desire. This was about souls recognizing each other, about love that refused to be contained by conventional boundaries.

Samaya pulled them closer, until they could feel each other's warmth, each other's breath. "I love you," she said, looking between them. "Both of you. Completely. Without reservation."

"I love you too," Valouna whispered, the words coming easier than she'd expected. "Both of you. And I'm trembling with fear. Samee, can you be content loving only us, for the rest of your life. We tried once, but I was only in it for you. Now I find myself loving John just as much as I love you."

"I promise to make you happy, just as much as I make John happy." Samee replied with pure hunger.

John's voice was thick with emotion when he spoke. "I still think both of you have a demonic pair of legs. But still, I love you both, more than I thought my heart was capable of holding."

They stood there in the moonlight, three hearts beating in imperfect but beautiful synchrony, finally brave enough to claim the love they'd found in each other. The future stretched before them, uncertain but no longer lonely, no longer halflived.

Outside, the night held its breath, as if the universe itself was honoring this moment of choosing love over fear, connection over solitude, hope over the safety of keeping their hearts locked away.

Whatever came next, they would face it together.

Samee once again, went and sat at the edge of the bed, overwhelming emotions turn her eyes into the Nile River. Valouna rushing to Samaya's side and gathering her into her arms. Samaya clung to her desperately, her tears soaking into Valouna's shirt as she released all the pain and confusion she'd been holding inside.

"Shh... It's okay. We're going to love you forever." Valouna's voice was soothing, her hand stroking Samaya's hair with infinite tenderness.

John approached more slowly, his footsteps soft on the plush carpet. He settled on the edge of the bed, his hand coming to rest on Samaya's shoulder. The touch was gentle, reassuring—a promise without words.

The room filled with quiet intimacy, the tension that had stretched between them replaced by something softer, more tender. This felt right in a way that defied logic or convention. It was messy, complicated, and probably impossible, but it was theirs.

Samaya lifted her head, her eyes red and swollen from crying. She looked between John and Valouna, her lips parting as if to speak, but instead of words, her hands moved to the buttons of Valouna's blouse.

Her fingers were trembling but reverent as she worked each button free, sliding the silk fabric off Valouna's shoulders to reveal the soft skin beneath. Valouna's breath came in slow, shallow waves, her body relaxing into the familiar intimacy.

John watched, his throat tight with desire and something deeper— love, recognition, acceptance. When Samaya turned to him, her eyes searching his face for permission, he nodded.

Understanding passed between them without words.

Samaya's smile was soft and tentative as she reached for him, her hands roaming over his chest, testing the boundaries of this new configuration. John closed his eyes, surrendering to the moment, to the undeniable connection between the three of them.

The air in the room grew warmer, more charged, as Samaya and Valouna continued their slow exploration of each other's bodies. There was no rush, no urgency—just the steady, deliberate rediscovery of familiar territory made new by the presence of a third heart, a third set of hands, a third soul joining their constellation.

John's hesitation melted away as he reached out, joining their embrace. His hands mapped the landscape of their skin, gentle but certain, as he allowed himself to become part of this moment of love, desire, and acceptance.

Their bodies and hearts intertwined in a dance that felt both natural and inevitable, three separate beings becoming something greater than the sum of their parts. The room filled with soft sounds—whispered confessions, gentle moans, the rustle of skin against skin—as they lost themselves in each other.

In the amber light of Samaya's bedroom, they found not just a physical connection but something deeper: the recognition that love, real love, doesn't always follow the rules society writes for it. Sometimes it's messier, more complex, more honest than anyone expects.

Sometimes it requires three hearts to beat as one.

Time seemed to slow as they moved together, each touch deliberate and meaningful. Samaya's tears had dried, replaced by something luminous—a joy so pure it seemed to radiate from her skin. She moved between John and Valouna like a conductor orchestrating a symphony, bringing their hands together, guiding their movements until the three of them existed in perfect harmony.

"I never thought..." Valouna whispered against Samaya's neck, her voice breaking with emotion. "I never thought I could feel this complete."

John's response was wordless, his lips finding the curve of Valouna's shoulder as his hand traced patterns on Samaya's back. The gesture was tender, reverent—a prayer written in touch. The weight of his years, the cynicism that had built up like scar tissue around his heart, melted away under the warmth of their combined presence.

Samaya turned in their embrace, her eyes meeting John's in the dim light. "You're not too old," she murmured, John's earlier words. "You're exactly who we need you to be."

Her hand cupped his face, thumb tracing the lines that spoke of laughter and sorrow, of a life fully lived. When she kissed him, it was with a gentleness that made his chest ache with gratitude. Behind her, Valouna's arms encircled them both, creating a cocoon of warmth and acceptance.

The night deepened around them as they explored this new language of love—one that required three voices to speak fluently. They learned the rhythm of each other's breathing, the subtle signs of pleasure and comfort, the way their bodies fit together in configurations that felt both surprising and inevitable.

John found himself amazed by his own capacity for tenderness, watching as Valouna and Samaya moved together with the fluid grace of lovers who had learned each other's secrets. When Valouna reached for him, drawing him closer, he felt something long-frozen in his chest finally thaw.

"I love watching you two together," Samaya breathed, her eyes dark with desire and affection as she observed John and Valouna's tentative exploration of each other. "You're beautiful."

The admission hung in the air like a blessing, permission to want what they had been afraid to acknowledge. John's hand found the back of Valouna's neck, drawing her into a kiss that tasted of discovery and promise. Her response was immediate, eager, as if she had been waiting for this moment without knowing it.

Samaya curled against them both, her lips trailing soft kisses along their shoulders, their necks, anywhere she could reach. The three of them moved in a slow dance of give and take, of whispered endearments and gentle laughter when someone's elbow found an inconvenient angle or when hair got tangled in eager fingers.

"We're going to have to figure out the logistics," Valouna said with a breathless laugh, her head pillowed on John's chest while Samaya traced idle patterns on her bare back.

"Like, who gets the good pillow?" Samaya teased, pressing a kiss to the spot between Valouna's shoulder blades.

"Like everything," John said, his voice rough with exhaustion and contentment. "But we will. We'll figure it all out."

The certainty in his voice surprised even him. This man, who had spent decades avoiding complications, was suddenly willing to embrace the most complicated situation imaginable. But as he looked down at the two women who had somehow managed to crack open his carefully guarded heart, he knew he would do whatever it took to make this work.

The moon had shifted in the sky, casting new patterns of light and shadow across their intertwined bodies. They talked in whispers about small things—whose apartment had the better kitchen, whether three people could realistically share a bathroom, how they would explain this to friends and family. The mundane concerns of real life were discussed with the wonder of people who had discovered something precious and rare.

"What happens tomorrow?" Valouna asked, her voice small in the darkness.

"Tomorrow we wake up," Samaya said simply. "And we choose each other again. And then we do it the day after that, and the day after that."

"Really, It's that simple?" John asked, though his tone suggested he hoped it could be.

"It's not that complicated," Samaya corrected with a soft smile. "But yes, it may not be that simple. As long I have you two, nothing else will mean more."

As dawn began to creep through the curtains, ready to fall asleep, bodies curved around each other like pieces of a puzzle, finally finding their proper places. The world outside might not understand what they had found, but in the sanctuary of Samaya's bedroom, three hearts beat in quiet synchrony, finally whole.

"Before you both fall asleep, and start dreaming about me. I need to tell you both a statement and a secret."

Valou and Samee look at each other intrigued. "Ok, you have our undivided attention."

"Yes, my baby, tell us." Samee added.

"As of last week, I quit my job and open my own Private Airline company with our initials as the name. I call it, JSV Airlines LLC."

Samee and Valou detangled themselves from John with delight, as they repeatedly kiss him all over his face. Joy flowing through them like electricity as they got up and jump up and down on the bed. They begin to imagine all their powerful connections from the modeling world they know, who would love to use their private airline. They also thought of marketing.

"Every month me and you are going to do, one major photoshoot with the top of the top photographers on the planet." Valou yelled out excitedly to Samee.

"We have to go to Vegas, and photograph by Mr. Luxury Media himself." Samee responded. As they both grab each other's hands and simultaneously screamed. "Marley Domeck-kkkk." Samee pause for a few seconds, look down at John. "Wait a minute, didn you say, you also have a statement to tell us."

With sincerity, John opens his mouth and spoke. "It's true we have lots to figure out. But no matter what bed we are on, the good pillow will always be mine."

Shock by John's statement, they both jump on him and tickled him to death. Some say he's still being tickled right now. Some say he woke up, wishing he was back asleep.

The End

Threefold Desire
"5 Years, Not One Dress Bought"

Yesterday I went shopping,

I saw a beautiful dress on a mannequin.

It made me think of you,

how beautiful you would look wearing it.

I'll do whatever it takes to buy it,

cuz you deserve the best,

I can see you wearing it now

but you don't even exist.

But this dress fits you perfect.

The type, you can work in,

or wear to red carpet events

with stage curtains.

The stitching is impeccable.

The fabric is exceptional.

It shows up at your doorstep,

that's my way of addressing you.

I know when you put it on,

you gonna love the way it fits.

I can see you posing in the mirror,

but you don't even exist.

it's the type of dress that's,

easy to be spotted in like polka dots.

The colors bring out

the beauty in your eyes

like photoshop.

The pattern will make you feel youthful.

The flow will make you feel pristine.

When you walk in a room,

you'll feel like you're in a Vogue magazine.

Running through an open field, in slow motion,

full of bliss.

Running to my arms

but you don't even exist

this dress is so nice

I have to take you to a ball for the night.

You take a million pictures

until you find that one You truly like

I got it just cause it's Tuesday

no special occa. Actions speak

actually, this dress makes that statement

I can't wait

until you see how pretty it is

My goals for my life

Is to witness first hand

All your Surprise expressions

but you don't even exist

it's the type of dress that

you would have me sit on the couch

playing Al Green album

while you dancing around

Teasing me,

Better yet, dancing with our kids

in the living room

I'm watching football

ignoring everything that you do

but in reality

My attention is really all on you

I love watching bellavision

right now

my favorite channel is you in this dress

You would look so amazing

But My heart beats in pain

Cause, you don't even exist

it's the type of dress that

I wouldn't even look at the tag

Cuz happiness has no price

so really why should I ask?

It's all purpose

so you wear it every chance you get

I'll buy it in 4 colors

to match your top 4 favorite bags

It's The type of dress

you absolutely would wear

When I pull up in my convertible car

head to a romantic picnic in central park.

This is the type of dress you wear

to show how happy you are

Or show me

None of them chicks are competition for you by far

every time you think, I'm not acting right

yesterday i went shopping

And time itself stop

When I spotted this beautiful dress

Instantly my heart

felt warm and gooey

it made me think of you

The win win

That's you in this dress

I couldn't resist, I swear…

I can see you vividly wearing it right now

With a beautiful smile

like you wanted me to write a poem about your smile next

As I took my card out to pay

my heart reverted back to the beats of reality

You would have been Iconic poetry

wearing this dress

But you don't even exist

Don't Quit Life

AKA

Jerry Calonge